Readers love
CATT FORD

Bulldozed

"I really loved this and I'm hoping more Western writers take a cue from Catt Ford and exchange tired Brokeback tributes for a little flamboyant pride more suited to the twenty-first century."
—Inked Rainbow Reads

The Cage

"*The Cage* by Catt Ford is a wonderfully kinky, sexy and erotic story of a group of friends who find love, laughter and happiness."
—Prism Book Alliance

"This story really shows how friends become family, one of which I really wouldn't mind being a part."
—The Blogger Girls

Bullheaded

"Catt Ford has given us many fully developed characters with real flaws and given us a set of MCs who are very REAL."
—Open Book Skye Reviews

"…*Bullheaded* is an enjoyable story that is sure to appeal to readers who enjoy romances set among the rough and tumble world of rodeos."
—Smexy Books

By CATT FORD

Bulldozed
Bullheaded
Bully for You
The Cage
Cross My Heart
With Sean Kennedy: Dash and Dingo
Extreme Bull
Hook, Line, and Sinker
The Last Concubine
Lily White Rose Red
Long Way Home
Murder at the Rocking R
Riding Out the Bull
A Strong Hand
Summer Fever
The Untold Want

Published by DREAMSPINNER PRESS
www.dreamspinnerpress.com

CATT FORD

CROSS MY HEART

DREAMSPINNER
PRESS

Published by
DREAMSPINNER PRESS

5032 Capital Circle SW, Suite 2, PMB# 279, Tallahassee, FL 32305-7886 USA
www.dreamspinnerpress.com

Cross My Heart
© 2017 Catt Ford.

Cover Art
© 2017 Catt Ford.
Cover content is for illustrative purposes only and any person depicted on the cover is a model.

ISBN: 978-1-63533-101-1
Digital ISBN: 978-1-63477-570-0
Library of Congress Control Number: 2016914559
Published February 2017
v. 1.0

Printed in the United States of America

This paper meets the requirements of
ANSI/NISO Z39.48-1992 (Permanence of Paper).

To JLC for making all things possible. Without you, this story would not have been written.

CHAPTER 1

DANIEL TOOK great pleasure in watching people, even though hope was dying for finding the one to inspire him to paint again.

Until he saw her.

The first time, her confident stride caught his eye. Attracted by her long legs and perfect derriere, he followed along in a desultory way until he lost sight of her in the crowd.

She must live or work somewhere near his *arrondissement*, because he kept spotting her. Daniel hadn't seen her face yet, but he admired her figure and the way she dressed. Like most Parisian women, she had that street-chic thing down. While her clothes were simple, they fit exceptionally well.

She probably wasn't avoiding him purposely; it was simply one of those frustrating quirks of fate that she always seemed to vanish before he caught up. She couldn't possibly know how much he wanted to see her face.

The colorful scarf she usually wore helped draw Daniel's attention to her. Her hair wasn't tortured to stick straightness. Instead, dark waves danced in the temperamental spring breeze as she moved, her stride long and energetic. Maybe the sun dazzled his eyes, but he thought he caught a glint of purple highlights. If only he could get close enough to check without alarming her.

Some might call him a stalker or obsessive, but ever since… *it*… happened, Daniel preferred not to get too close to his fellow beings. Watching them from afar was sufficient.

Even Daniel wasn't sure exactly what he was searching for, but he hoped he'd know it when he saw it. Purely physical beauty did not satisfy him. He wanted something more, a quirk of personality or a hint of the inner spirit. Even a crooked smile might do the trick.

Ironically, now that Daniel had enough money to be able to paint anything he wanted, his muse had deserted him. If only he could catch up with this girl and she sparked his fancy, Daniel was sure he would be able to paint again. If he could convince her to sit for him.

Today she carried a large, flat portfolio, and the breeze lifted it like a sail, pulling her quickly along the pavement. Daniel tried to work his way through the throng of people without stepping on toes or elbowing ribs to get close enough for a good look. She laughed to herself as she turned to wrestle the errant portfolio back under control. For one breathless moment, the world stood still and their eyes met.

She was lovelier than he'd hoped, but not only for her cheekbones and eyes. In that one quick flash, he felt as if her essence had been laid bare to him, all the imperfections and fears, but more importantly the indomitable spirit of her being. Everything about her, the way she moved and the curve of her lips, said that if he was lucky enough to know her, life would be full of pleasant and interesting surprises.

In that split second of awareness, Daniel saw her and he knew she saw him. Then the wind caught her hair and tossed it playfully into her face. She reached up to smooth a strand behind her ear and turned away as if their souls had not just touched. Apparently unmoved by the moment they'd shared, she crossed the street with the rest of the pedestrians.

She was the one. He had to paint her. If only he could do justice to her. Shaken by the glance they exchanged, he doubted his own ability to capture what he'd seen, but he had to try.

Standing immobile on the pavement, buffeted by the hurrying crowd, Daniel let her slip away and disappear.

Damn. So that's what it feels like.

A PRICKLE of awareness made Lana wary. Someone was watching her. Perhaps overly sensitive, but she'd learned the hard way to be vigilant. She had been followed before.

The day the wind caught her portfolio and spun her around, she realized she'd seen that man on the street before. He hadn't triggered an alarm in her before this. His face was classically handsome and his eyes were a heavenly shade of blue. His neatly cut light brown hair gave him a conservative appearance. Nothing to make him stand out in a crowd except for the way he stared. As if he'd been struck by lightning.

Since that day, Lana had seen him twice more. Each time, Lana managed to avoid him, but he was persistent. At first she thought it coincidence that their paths kept crossing. This part of the city was crowded, and she recognized other people on the street occasionally, although she didn't actually know them.

Today had been close, though. The man had almost caught up this time. If he did, he might even try to speak to her.

Without a moment to spare, Lana darted inside her apartment building, hoping the man was far enough behind to miss which doorway she'd entered. Before the door closed behind her, Lana eluded the chatty landlady and raced up the stairs. Six flights to the top floor and then down the dingy hallway to her apartment.

Her hand shook slightly as she inserted the key in the lock. She was panting, and it wasn't the stairs. Once inside, Lana locked the door and leaned against it to catch her breath.

Then she went into the lounge and flopped down onto the sofa. Lana didn't turn on a lamp although it was growing dark. No sense in escaping the man and then flashing a beacon if he'd managed to figure out which building she'd entered.

If he was actually following her. She could be imagining his interest, and she didn't want to examine the reason too closely. Possibly because she found the man attractive rather than threatening.

When she was younger, the sight of a man on her trail could trigger a full-blown panic, but Lana had become used to attracting attention, if only for her height. Lana had learned how to forestall casual encounters, but this was the third time, and she realized he was definitely following her.

Something drew Lana to this particular man… and so far, she hadn't been able to put her finger on why. It wasn't simply his appearance. By now she'd learned to pass attractive men on the street without a tremor. No sense pining over what she couldn't have, but this time her body kept betraying her.

Lana usually kept rigid control over her thoughts and desires. If she gave in to desire, the yearning to be held, kissed, or even more, the walls she'd built might come tumbling down, especially after being celibate for so long. She was definitely better off alone. She already knew the risks, and experience had taught her not to expect a good outcome.

Lana had her work and her friends. Her lips twisted in a wry smile. Somehow the thought of them was not as comforting as usual.

Impatiently Lana kicked off her shoes, as if the man below could hear her heels tapping on the parquet floor. If he was actually still out there. She rose and crossed to the window to check, standing where the curtain concealed her but she could see out. And there he was.

But was he there for her? He walked slowly along the pavement, scanning the buildings on both sides of the street as if looking for an address. Lana hoped the man didn't know where she lived, but if he was following her and he'd gotten this far, it would be only a matter of time.

Tall and imposing, the man was casually dressed in a leather jacket and jeans. When she'd looked into his eyes on the street, his expression seemed gentle to her, at odds with his tenacity in following her. Stroking her throat with one finger, Lana watched him meander along the street. How long would he wait out there?

A loud bang made her jump. Then she laughed in the silence of her apartment. She ought to be used to the sound of the radiator by now.

She forced herself away from the window. She could make coffee. Or turn on the television. Reorganize her wardrobe. But instead of doing something useful to get her mind off the man,

Lana went back to the window to watch him. He was still looking up at the windows, first on one side of the street and then the other. When he turned to scrutinize her building, Lana drew back behind the curtains as if he had the ability to see through brick and mortar.

Lana jumped again when she heard a knock at her door. The man was still down there, so it wasn't him. Lana went silently to the door. "Qui est là?" she called out in a low voice.

"C'est moi." The answer came in Dom's familiar voice.

Lana unlocked the door and opened it a slit to peek out. "What are you doing here?"

"I WAS in the neighborhood and thought I'd drop by." Dom pushed the door open and squeezed past her into the foyer. "Why the third degree?" Then he did a double take at her suit. "What the hell are you wearing?"

She looked down at her ensemble. "I should think it was obvious. It's a suit."

"A man's suit? With a tie?"

"It's ironic, Dominick. Menswear translated into women's fashion is almost a trope, it's been so done, but I hope you didn't come by to discuss my outfit. My vocation bores you, remember?"

"I came by to remind you that Colin changed the dinner to tomorrow instead of Friday. Something about his girlfriend's schedule. And because I like seeing you." His irritation turned to concern when Lana crossed the darkened room to the window and looked down at the street. "What's up?"

"You didn't have to remind me. I have it marked on my calendar."

"You mean your assistant Catharine marked it out for you. Usually you forget until the last minute, although not if there's a chance to show off a new outfit." Dom turned on a lamp and noticed she flinched at the sudden light. She hadn't seemed as nervous in quite some time, and he felt a twinge of alarm. "Why are you sitting in the dark?"

"Standing, actually." Lana gestured out the window. "One of my hordes of admirers followed me home. Perhaps."

Dom hurried over and looked out. "The guy walking back and forth?" At her nod, he moved slightly in front of her and peered around the edge of the curtain. "You're sure it's you the bloke's after?"

"No, not at all. Shall I go down and ask him?" Lana shrugged. "Perhaps we could invite him to come up and join us for a coffee. I was about to make some."

"Are you daft?" Dom demanded. "You're not thinking of talking to him!"

"If he's truly following me, I should think he'll soon be talking to me. He can't be doing it simply for practice. Unless he's a detective or something like that. But perhaps he's merely looking for an address."

"You don't seem to be taking this too seriously." Dom was worried and Lana didn't seem worried enough, although she was obviously unsettled.

"Well, it's exciting in a way, isn't it?" Lana stared down at the man. "He's very handsome. Perhaps he's developed a grand passion for me."

Dom glanced out the window again and bristled. Anyone who followed Lana couldn't look good to him no matter how attractive, and he was perfectly willing to believe the worst of the guy without any evidence. "I don't think he's all that handsome."

Lana shook her head. "Not your type at all."

"Nor yours, if you know what's good for you. You have no idea who he is. Or what he's after." His anxiety soared from zero to one hundred. Dom clamped his teeth together. Now he needed to find out: What was the man doing there?

"If it's me he's following, now he knows approximately where I live. If he wants to confront me, it's inevitable that we'll be having a conversation." Lana tensed her shoulders. "Unless this is all a figment of my overactive imagination."

"If you say anything at all to him, tell him to fuck off!"

"Well, who died and left you in charge, you cockwomble?"

"Yeah, that's me." Dom had to grin at her colorful way of putting it but forged ahead anyway. "Listen, I worry about you."

"I know you do." Lana sighed, her exasperation obvious. "If I need help, you'll be my first call."

"You stay away from him," Dom ordered.

"Dom, you're a dick." Lana took off her coat and dropped it on the couch. She wrapped her arms around herself. "You're not the boss of me."

"Someone should be," Dominick snapped. "Someone ought to put you on a leash so you'd be safe crossing the streets."

"Somebody has a high opinion of himself."

"Moi?" Innocently, Dom tilted his head and put his hand on his chest.

"Pitre." She scowled at him. "If he does try to talk to me, I shall tell him I'm not interested."

"Just try to avoid him altogether until I have a chance to find out who he is. I'm good at this, Lana. It's my job. You can leave that bit to me."

"Don't waste your time, Dom. So far we're not even sure if it was really me he was after."

"It's not a waste." Dom curled his hands into fists. Maybe he'd go down there and confront the man right now. Get this over with right quick.

Lana pulled Dom into a hug and rested her chin on the top of his head. "Thank you for caring about me so much, but you have to get past it."

"Have you?" Dom pulled away and searched her eyes for the hurt she hid so well. "Some things you don't ever get past no matter how hard you try to lay them to rest."

"You're right, that was glib. But we can't stress out over every little thing out of the ordinary. I'm fine. Some definition of fine. Very likely that gentleman has merely come to visit a friend and was trying to find the right place. His being down there may have absolutely nothing to do with me."

Dom managed to pry his clenched teeth apart. "I suppose we are being a bit overly vigilant, but I'll have a look at him in any case. You weren't planning to go back out again tonight, were you?"

"Do I ever?" Lana's tone was bitter, but she reached out and tried to pat his head.

"Quit that. You know I hate it. And no, you don't go out much."

"I was planning to go to bed soon anyway. I have an early day tomorrow."

"All right. I'll see what I can find out. And I'll be around when you go to work tomorrow, to see if he's hanging about."

"Skulking."

"Definitely skulking."

"Thank you."

Dom walked to the door and put his hand on the knob. "Bolt the door after me."

"Of course," she said.

Waiting only long enough to hear the click of the deadbolt, Dom ran down to the ground floor, his footsteps ringing in the narrow staircase in his rush. He was *not* going to fail Lana again.

The rational part conceded she might be correct. Coincidence might have led the man to her street after she'd noticed him earlier. If he lived nearby, their paths might cross any number of times and it would be perfectly random and legitimate.

Dom knew quite a few of his neighbors by sight, simply due to proximity. With real estate at a premium, almost everyone lived cheek by jowl, and Dom was always trying to duck one rather relentless woman who showed signs she desired more togetherness that he.

But Dom was not going to leave this one to coincidence. If this man was stalking Lana, Dom would put a stop to it. Dark thoughts about how he might accomplish that almost drove him out into the street to collar the bastard straightaway. Still, Dom took his time, holding the outer door to Lana's building open slightly to peer out to locate the man.

What Dom saw was the man's back. He'd strolled up and down the street several times while Dom and Lana watched, but now he'd apparently given up. Waiting only until the man was out of sight, Dom shot out of Lana's building and ran after him as quietly as he could. At the end of the street, Dom flattened himself against the corner of the last building and peeked around it. Apparently unaware of Dom's presence, the man was in no hurry. He went on his way at normal speed. Feeling a bit of a fool for his dramatic action-movie turn, Dom followed.

Rage boiled up inside Dom again and he wanted to run up to the man, slam him up against a building until his eyes rolled back in his head, and beat the answer out of him. The fact that the man was taller and heavier meant nothing. No one was ever going to hurt Lana again. Not on his watch! The vow he'd taken had no witnesses, but Dom was determined to keep her safe, if only as penance for his previous shortcomings.

The man stopped suddenly to look into a shop window. Dom hurried to a news kiosk and grabbed a newspaper to cover his face, tapping his foot impatiently before he risked a peek around the edge.

Eventually the man moved on and entered a café. Dom followed him inside. This would be his chance to examine the man's face in case he needed to describe him later. Realizing he couldn't sit at the counter without ordering, Dom asked for a bowl of soup. He wasn't hungry, but he ate anyway without a clue as to what kind he'd gotten. Who knew how long this chase might take? He wasn't going to lose the man by going faint from hunger.

Dom started to compile a description in his head. The man was tall, at least six feet. Obviously foreign—takes one to know one—quintessentially all-American good looks. Slightly too muscular to qualify as metrosexual. His clothing was characterized by a rugged chic, sporty but with a polish probably acquired in Paris. His face was clean-shaven and he filled out a pair of jeans well, a feature that Dom should not be looking at right now.

And yet the smug, self-conscious look in the man's eyes roused Dom's suspicions. He was no innocent tourist. His presence on Lana's street was not a coincidence. Dom waited impatiently as the man lingered over his meal. Dom had already paid for his own in order to be ready when the man left. If Dom could only follow the guy to his address, that would be enough to get the research started. Then he would have a better idea of how much trouble Lana was in.

Finally, the man paid his bill and left. While Dom dawdled outside the café, a taxi suddenly appeared. The man raised his arm to flag it. The driver slammed on the brakes and swerved to the curb, and the man got in.

Dom ran the two blocks to the nearest taxi stand, but before he reached it, the man's taxi was out of sight. Not beaten yet, Dom fell into the first cab in the ranks, handed over some euros, and directed the driver to turn the same corner the man's cab had. "Follow that cab" didn't have quite the same ring in French, but he got his point across. However, by the time the driver had laboriously turned his taxi around, the other cab was long gone, leaving Dom to fume in disgust.

Of course he couldn't be sure, but the man must have twigged him. Dom hated to admit it, but he could have sworn he saw the man turn around and grin while the cab bore him away.

How could he face Lana and admit he'd lost the man? Dom didn't even care about making good on his boasts. The important thing was to prevent anyone from getting to her. He smacked his right fist into his left hand. The taxi driver glanced at him with concern in the rearview mirror, and Dom sighed. Defeated for now, he gave the driver his own address and settled back for the ride.

HUNGER DROVE Daniel from his post. Apparently she was not planning to come out again that evening, but at least he now knew the street she lived on, even if he didn't yet know her name. Tomorrow was another day, and he needed to fill his inner emptiness—with food at least, as there was nothing else on offer.

As he turned the corner, the hair stood up on the back of his neck. Having learned the hard way not to ignore his instincts, Daniel took a casual glance behind him when he rounded the next corner. Sure enough, a man was following him. He forced the rush of adrenaline down and kept walking while he decided what to do. First things first. Was the man really following him? Daniel stopped in front of a handy cheese shop and watched for his shadow in the reflection in the window. The man stopped when he did, and retreated to a news kiosk. He pretended to look at the papers while watching Daniel around the edge of one. Amateur.

Daniel started off again and the man followed immediately. Daniel could sniff out the police eight blocks away, and this was no cop, not even a French one. Detective? Undercover? No, a professional would surely be better than this. While his brain raced trying to figure out why he could have attracted anyone's interest, Daniel amused himself by periodically darting off to look into shop windows in order to gloat over the consternation of his shadow. Then he snapped his fingers with sudden realization.

The man was probably a reporter. Daniel had had enough of them following him in New York after...*it*... happened. He had come to Europe to escape their attention, but now it seemed one of them was onto him again. His story was so old and unimportant, Daniel had hoped they were onto newer scandals and he could live in peace.

Now that he knew someone was on his trail again, Daniel would be on his guard. A noisy growl from his stomach reminded him that he was hungry. He entered a small café at random and took a seat. Daniel had nothing to hide. Not anymore. Besides, he was good enough to dodge one solo reporter if that's who it was.

Daniel enjoyed his meal all the more for watching the man suck down a cup of soup at the counter in a hurry. He memorized the man's appearance, just in case. On the short side of average, nondescript face except for a pug nose, medium brown hair.

After he ate and paid his bill, Daniel left the restaurant and, by an extraordinary stroke of luck, managed to flag down a taxi on the quiet street. The look of chagrin on the reporter's face when he was left flat-footed to stare after the cab kept Daniel chuckling quietly to himself all the way home, but when he arrived safely, he wasn't laughing anymore. He made sure no one was waiting for him before he entered his building. He'd won this round, but he would see that reporter again. He was sure of it.

Then a sudden realization hit him. If he felt threatened by the reporter behind him, how would that beautiful girl feel if she noticed him following her? He was in good shape and able to take care of himself. She was more vulnerable. Stalking her was not going to endear him to her. He was ashamed he had taken so long to think of her side of it. He'd been so wound up in the hope of painting again, he hadn't given her reaction a thought.

If he was ever going to have a chance with her, he needed to back off. But if he did, how could he meet her? Daniel had no idea who she was. The idea of approaching her was exhilarating and terrifying at the same time. He would have to think about it, but to start with, Daniel resolved never to go near the street where she lived again. Unless invited, of course. But if he didn't know her, how could she invite him? His brain hopped onto the hamster wheel and started it spinning. He didn't get much sleep that night.

WHEN DOM finally pried himself away, Lana bolted the door after him in relief.

She really hadn't needed that added little bit of drama Dom always seemed to stir up. She went back to the window. The man had apparently given up. He was walking west to the end of the block. Then he turned right. Lana waited. After a minute she spied Dom following the man in a suitably surreptitious manner, skulking as he'd promised. Lana rolled her eyes when she saw Dom flatten himself against a building and then sneak around the corner. She drew the curtains, hoping Dom would not call her tonight with the results of his playing detective. If the phone did ring, she would feel obligated to answer to prevent Dom rushing back over here to make sure she was alive.

Lana picked up her shoes and carried them to the bedroom. It was tucked behind a partial wall and furnished with furniture she'd found at the flea market.

The headboard was upholstered in velvet, and a silk duvet covered the bed, lending a bit of luxury to the secondhand pieces. Lana stored her shoes neatly away in the mirrored wardrobe. Early on she'd discovered living in such limited space required organization and constant policing, difficult when paired with an addiction to clothes. She took off her suit and hung it on a padded hanger. Lingerie went into the hamper.

She went down the narrow hall leading to the bathroom. A pedestal sink shared the microscopic space with the toilet and shower, but a bathtub had been sacrificed for the practicality of a washer. The frosted glass window let in light while still guarding her privacy.

Although small, the flat was the first place she'd ever had all to herself. Lana loved the beauty and tranquility she'd created. The only thing that would have made it better was someone to share it with, but that dream was impossible.

Quickly, Lana removed her makeup and bent over the sink to wash. She buried her face in the towel for a moment and then looked up at the mirror to see herself stripped bare.

"Hello, Roland." His voice was soft and husky. "Nice to see you again."

Roland reached for a jar of moisturizer. As he started to smooth the cream onto his skin, he closed his eyes and pretended it was another man's hands roaming over his body. Not just any man, he realized. The hands Roland wanted to feel on his skin were those of the handsome man who'd followed him. The man might prove to be dangerous, but he was sexy as hell. Roland kept thinking about the man even though there was no point. Roland tried to forget him and concentrate on the usual faceless, nameless hero of his imagination. He wrapped his arms around himself in a tender embrace, but tonight the fantasy of happily ever after wasn't working. That castle in the air dissolved into his lonely reality. After one last try, Roland opened his eyes to be confronted with the reality of him groping himself. He sneered at himself in the mirror.

"L'amour. Le bullshit. Pathetic."

He returned to the bedroom, put on a negligée, and went to bed.

CHAPTER 2

ALTHOUGH IT was a wrench to alter her routine, Lana stayed away from her favorite café for a week. She walked to work by a different route and watched out for the handsome man but never saw him.

Two days later she met Dom in a different café for morning coffee. "Well?"

"And a good morning to you, Lana. I thought you didn't care whether I followed him."

"I don't, but I know you were keen to do it." Lana took a sip of her coffee and made a face.

"Coffee snob."

"So sue me. Henri's coffee is better. So what did you find out?" Lana abandoned pretense. Dom was a tease not telling her right out.

A rich red bloomed over Dom's face. "I lost him."

"I beg your pardon? I didn't quite hear that." Smirking at his discomfiture, Lana put a hand up to her ear. "I thought you said this is what you do, this is what you're good at—"

"Ha-ha, I get it, very amusing. Mock me while you can. Well, this time I wasn't such a hotshot. I lost him. He hailed a cab."

Lana was surprised. "Where, on the street?"

"Yeah, go figure. You never see an empty cab roaming anywhere in Paris, and all of a sudden, he manages to nick one. I had to run to a stand, and by the time I found one, he was gone. He escaped my eagle eye. He won, I lost."

Lana took a bite of her roll and chewed. "He was probably just lost when he was on my street."

"But I'm not licked yet."

15

She put her roll down. "And just what do you plan to do? Is there a directory I don't know about for good-looking men where you enter their stats: light brown hair and blue eyes—"

"That would be awesome, wouldn't it? Blue eyes, eh? I thought you weren't taking that much notice of him."

The knowing leer on Dom's face rankled, but Lana refused to let him know how much. "I merely happened to notice, that's all. So what's your deep, dark plan now?"

"I'll just follow you myself, and if he really is after you, he'll show up again, don't you think?"

"And I'm sure your employer will certainly be charmed to pay you to stand guard over me."

"I'm not planning to cover you 24/7 round the clock, see?" Dom assumed a shifty-eyed sneer and darted a glance around the café. "I figure this way, if a fella has the hots for a dame, he won't give up, see? He'll sniff out the trail—no, I mean, he'll shadow you either on the way to or from work, and when—"

She could almost see the imaginary cigarette dangling from the corner of his mouth. "Dom, pick one. Hard-boiled 1940s private dick or cowboy. You're mixing your metaphors."

"You're making fun of me."

"I'm trying just as hard as I can."

They glared at each other. The way Dom thrust his lower lip out in a pugnacious pout always made her laugh, and Lana felt it coming on. She bit the inside of her cheek to stifle a giggle.

"I talked to Terry and Colin. They'll each take a shift. Colin on mornings, Terry at night. So you're covered."

"Thanks, I'll try not to give you guys the slip. See?"

"As if you could."

"Don't tempt me."

Dom got serious. "I'm not going to tempt you. I just want to keep you safe."

The look in his eyes reminded Lana of a time she didn't like thinking about, but she was touched anyway. "Thank you, Dom. I'll be good."

He heaved a deep sigh. "You always are, Lana. And I'm sorry you have to be."

"DAMMIT!"

Daniel threw his paintbrush across the room into the sink. Two points. Except who the hell cared? He stared at his unfinished canvas. He was well trained; his mentor had seen to that. He knew he was talented; art reviews in the newspaper said so, and the *Times* was never wrong. But that had been two years ago. Maybe he'd lost it. Maybe he couldn't paint any longer.

No, he knew he could still paint. Nothing had happened to his hands. And Daniel could still visualize the image of what he wanted to paint, the brush just refused to cooperate. Not that one fleeting glance at a crosswalk was sufficient for a portrait no matter how compelling the model. He was used to spending hours with his subjects. That was how Daniel got to know them, letting them talk while he listened and painted. He'd gotten a lot of action that way in the past. Rich society women whose husbands didn't understand and never listened.

This girl was different. Something unusual about her fascinated him. She was a mystery he wanted to solve, but slowly, to savor the answer to all of his questions. In fact, to hell with the painting. He wanted nothing more than to listen to whatever she wanted to tell him. Daniel needed that time to study the way light caressed the planes of her face and carved out shadows under her cheekbones. To memorize the exact slant of her eyes and gauge the depth of the hollows at her temples. To find out who she was. But how?

He wanted to hear her voice saying his name. Hell, he just wanted to hear her voice no matter what she said.

Daniel closed his eyes. When he opened them again, he examined his work with a critical eye. He'd tried to capture that split second when he first saw her face and their eyes met. Tried it. Failed. The beauty was there, and some of the spark of life in her eyes. As a quick sketch, it wasn't bad. He simply needed more time staring at her. A lot more time. He needed to know.

During the week that followed, Daniel tried to figure out a way he could approach the girl without scaring her. He avoided her street but as they lived in the same arrondissement, seeing her again was inevitable. It couldn't come soon enough for him.

Several disappointing days passed when he failed to see her at all, although he again caught sight of the pug-nosed reporter who had trailed him that night. Eventually Daniel learned which café she favored. To Daniel's surprise, the reporter joined the girl there for coffee and he realized they actually knew each other. That meeting gave Daniel a different idea about why the man followed him. The short man might not be a reporter at all. Maybe he was merely looking out for the girl. Although Daniel approved of that in principle, her shadow did make things more difficult for him.

Over the next two weeks, Daniel observed two other short men trailing the girl at different times, and once all four of them met at her café for lunch. His frustration built as he watched the easy camaraderie among them, wishing he could be at that table and accepted as one of the group. The realization dawned that these men were friends of hers and not lovers. Their attitude was more protective watchdog than beau. But how could he get past them?

In the end, Daniel decided on the direct approach. At least that way he would know where he stood. If he waited until she came to the café alone, he wouldn't be forced to run the gauntlet of her protective friends. He would approach her only if there were plenty of people around so she would feel safe. He would hear her voice at last.

CHAPTER 3

AFTER TWO long weeks of enduring Dom's presence behind her, Lana told him to give it up. She was alone again when she saw the man standing at a corner two blocks from her favorite café. She stopped short to consider the wisdom of going on or making her opinion known by fleeing in the opposite direction. But the man's goofy grin and the way he shifted nervously from one foot to the other told her that he would not pursue her if she told him to leave her alone. She didn't feel particularly threatened and the street was crowded with witnesses. Lana felt relieved that this confrontation was finally here, although she intended to make short work of him. He could tell her what he wanted and then she would send him on his way.

She slowed as she approached the intersection, and the man spoke to her.

He stammered slightly, as if trying to deliver his opening line in style. "Voyez le beau femme avec de longues jambes comme la tige d'une fleur."

With a polite smile, Lana replied in French: "Fuck off, you pervy asshole."

He chuckled and tried again. "Classy. Vous portez le danger comme un beau vêtement."

"Vous êtes américain?" Lana caught the slightly flat *r*'s, although the rest of his French was good enough.

"Is my accent that bad?" he asked, switching to English.

"No, it's rather good." She pounced on his mistake with glee. "But you used the masculine adjective *beau* instead of *belle*."

"Did I?" He smiled. "My apologies. Gendered articles and nouns always trip up the ugly American, is that it?"

"You're not so ugly that you should avoid direct sunlight." She glanced at him from the corner of her eye and turned away quickly when she realized he was watching. He was hard to ignore, but Lana tried not to smile. No point in encouraging him. The traffic light changed and she started across the intersection.

"Je vous ai observée—"

"I know." She smirked at his dismay. "I spotted you over a week ago."

"Busted. I hoped I'd been more careful than that. I didn't want to alarm you. I only wanted to talk to you."

"What have we to talk about?"

He cleared his throat. "There's an exciting aura of danger around you."

"Oh my. Do you get a lot of action with that tired old line?"

"You'd be surprised."

"I certainly would if you did, which I doubt."

"I wish I could paint you."

"What color?"

Daniel laughed at that. "Any color you like. You have the most beautiful mouth I've ever seen."

"That's better." Lana couldn't resist smiling at that. Compliments tended to be a bit sparse in her life. "But still a bit of a bore. Couldn't you compare them to the softness of rose petals or something more poetic?"

"I couldn't possibly until we share a kiss and I find out for myself how soft they are."

"Cheeky. Perhaps you'd better immortalize a different part of me, then. One you can admire from afar. An elbow, perhaps."

"How far afar?"

"Oh, from across the street at the very least. Preferably the length of a rugby pitch." She stood still, her hand out to keep him at a distance.

He raised his hands in surrender and took a step back. "No kiss, then?"

"No kiss."

"May I buy you a cup of coffee, then?"

Finally, she laughed at him. "From the sublime to the mundane. That at least has the merit of novelty."

"What?"

"The direct approach." Lana eyed him speculatively. "Why should I let a complete stranger buy me a coffee?"

"Strangers are only friends we haven't met yet." He scrubbed a hand over his face when she snickered. "I know, not my best effort, but I wish you would. If you say no, I promise to go away and eat worms and you'll never see me again."

"Worms? Whatever for?" She started walking again, and when he tagged along, she didn't tell him to leave her alone.

"Never mind. It's from an old song in America. I wanted to introduce myself and—" He cut off abruptly. "And see if you like your coffee as much as I do."

"Coffee is very important." She stopped in front of her café. At least the proprietor Henri knew her and would have her back if this man proved difficult. "This place is quite decent. If you like, you may come in, but afterwards you'd better run along. I'm busy."

"As long as you recommend it, I shall trust your judgment."

He seemed to be ignoring the running along part, but he'd soon realize she meant it. He opened the door for her. Lana shivered as his hand barely skimmed her back to guide her inside, and hoped she'd managed to keep the amused, slightly bored expression she'd perfected intact. She did not want to encourage him. To her relief, the café was predictably busy. Safety in numbers.

She went to the counter and greeted the proprietor. Henri looked both startled and pleased as he darted a meaningful glance at her temporary companion. To forestall any verbal encouragement from Henri, Lana ordered rapidly in French, without giving her admirer a chance to get a word in.

With a wry smile, the man shrugged and went to claim a table.

Lana joined him at the table at the window and left her coat on when she sat down. No point letting him think this would be a friendly breakfast to linger over, although the feeling of being on a date was rather novel. She suppressed that thought instantly. That way lay danger.

"Shall I like what we're getting?" He rested both arms on the table and slid down in his seat a little, slouching as many Americans tended to.

"You know perfectly well what I asked for. You speak French very well."

"Also German, Spanish, Italian…." He shrugged as though his linguistic talents were almost not worth mentioning.

Actually, Lana was impressed. So few Americans attempted to master even the basics of another language. "You have me topped, then. I speak only French and English."

"You speak French beautifully. I would have thought you were a native." He offered his hand. "My name is Daniel Hunter."

She ignored his hand. "Lana."

"As in Svetlana?" Showing no sign of discomfort, he withdrew his hand. "You remind me of a black orchid. Exotic, mysterious…."

Lana shook her head. "Oh, I don't like that."

"But why? It's pretty," Daniel said. "The Chinese word for orchid is *lan*."

"You speak Chinese too?"

He laughed. "Not fluently. I can ask where the bathroom is and say 'stupid melon head' in Mandarin, but that's about it. An old friend of mine was originally from Taipei. Lana, Lan. It was an easy jump. Why don't you like it? Orchids are beautiful."

"Black orchid reminds me of the Black Dahlia, that poor girl who was murdered in Hollywood in the forties." Lana studied his face. He was more interesting than she'd expected. How would he react to overt suspicion? Surely he was smart enough to expect hostility when approaching a perfect stranger. "Are you planning to kill me, Daniel?"

He warded off the thought with both hands. "Only with pleasure, if you'll allow it."

"I will certainly allow you to pay for breakfast if you wish, but that's all."

"I do wish, but I hope to do much more for you."

When the proprietor arrived at this opportune moment with their coffee, rolls, and butter, Lana thanked him. "Merci, Henri."

Henri bowed and smiled. Shifting slightly so his back was to Daniel, Henri gave her an encouraging wink before returning to his place behind the counter. Lana suppressed the urge to roll her eyes at Henri.

Daniel stirred sugar into his coffee and added cream. "If you don't like orchids, what about Snow White, then?"

"If I must have a nickname, at least that one has been mentioned before."

"It fits. Dark glossy hair, pale luminous skin. A face beautiful enough to steal a man's heart out of his chest." He took a sip of his coffee and nodded in surprised approval. "And you have at least three of the seven dwarfs tagging around after you, as well as me."

Lana didn't mean to giggle, but it escaped her. "You weren't supposed to notice them."

"They were right behind you. Hard to miss. May I ask who they are?"

"They like to think of themselves as the Three Musketeers."

"All for one and one for all?"

"Yes, but in keeping with Snow White, I call them Happy, Bashful, and Dopey."

Daniel laughed. "And are they?"

"Quite the opposite, actually. Happy is quite grumpy, Bashful swings from the chandeliers at his parties, and Dopey is actually, well, rather silly at that, but he's sweet." She leaned forward and whispered

confidentially. "He thinks wearing glasses makes him look smart."
What was she thinking? This man was not a friend. Yet.

"So they're not just following you about by chance."

"I noticed you following me and told them. They were trying to
follow you. Turnabout is fair play."

"I admit that's true, although I didn't know what else to do. It's
a little difficult to engineer a meeting without knowing your name or
a mutual acquaintance. Ex-boyfriends?"

Lana threw back her head and laughed at the thought. "Hardly.
Let's just say very old friends."

"And where are the other four?"

She lifted her hand a dismissive gesture. "I had to let them go.
They were such downers. Grumpy, Sleepy, Sleazy, and Spock."

"I believe it was Sneezy, Dancer, Prancer, and Doc." Daniel
counted silently on his fingers. "Wait a sec, I seem to have muddled a
few reindeer in there."

"Whatever. I kept the good dwarfs on and kicked the rest to the
curb." Lana realized too late she was warming to Daniel and babbling
her head off about things he didn't need to know.

"So if you agreed to go out with me…."

"We would have chaperones." She watched over the rim of her
coffee cup to gauge his reaction. Most men would object strenuously
to the idea of her friends trailing along. Instead he laughed and
shrugged.

"They're kind of short to be landing a punch if they're forced to
defend your honor." Daniel grinned.

"Not at all. The family jewels are at the perfect level for a well-
aimed blow, particularly from a dwarf." Lana took wicked pleasure
watching Daniel squirm in his seat. "But it's a moot point. My honor
is completely secure. I never see anyone."

"Neither do I. So we have that in common. Always a good sign,
having something in common right from the start."

"I'm a Leo."

"I didn't mean it quite that way, but I should have guessed from
the leonine hair. I am a Sagittarius."

"Ah, you like the thrill of the hunt."

Daniel looked her right in the eye, although he went scarlet in shame. "Yes, about that. I need to apologize. When I saw you and looked into your eyes…." Abruptly, Daniel abandoned that sentence and shook his head. "No excuses. I—I followed you without thinking about how you would feel about it. I didn't mean to scare you. I regret that and I apologize, but I didn't know how else to meet you."

"And now that we've met?"

The sound of a plate shattering on the tile floor made Lana stiffen. The sudden shock of noise cut through the din of other customers. During the moment of silence before the noise resumed, the insistent hammer of Lana's pulse roared in her ears, but she thought she covered her reaction well. When she looked at Daniel again, she thought she recognized the same expression in his eyes, although it was gone too fast to be sure.

Henri called out, "Je suis désolé, pardonnez l'accident."

Conversation at other tables went on as Henri cleaned up. Gradually Lana's heart rate slowed and her respiration returned to normal.

Daniel's nostrils flared as he sucked in an audible breath, but he smiled and carried on as if he'd shown no reaction at all. "I hope you'll accept my apology. Because if you don't, the only way to prove myself will be to go away, and I don't want to go away. If you say no, I'll have to accept it and it's worms for dinner for me." His eyes gleamed. "But we clicked, didn't we?"

She admired his ability to pick up the conversation after that shock. Lana studied his face for a long time before she smiled. The desire to conquer and acquire she saw from so many men seemed curiously absent. "Perhaps we did, but I'm serious. I have no interest in dating."

"Anyone, or only me?"

"Anyone at all."

"But you like men."

Lana looked away from him. "Maybe so, but that need not concern you, as we shall not be putting it to the test."

"At least I don't bore you."

"Only a little." Lana covered her mouth with her hand to hide a smile, knowing her remark would irk him. Already she realized not much escaped this man. He was intelligent and sensitive. As yet, she wasn't exactly sure what she wanted, but it would definitely be safer if he disappeared from her life.

"And here I thought I was more original than that." Daniel heaved a theatrical sigh. "Meet me for dinner tonight. You must eat anyway, why not with me? Of course it'll be a bit crowded with all the dwarfs along, but I'm sure we can get a bigger table."

"How lovely of you to offer to include them. And afterwards?"

"Whatever you like. We could all go to the cinema or for a group hike...."

"Or back to your place?" She couldn't quite keep the sarcastic note from her voice. Men had one-track minds, and she wasn't going to play along.

"Only if you beg really hard. And that's where I draw the line on the dwarfs coming along."

Lana laughed at the thought. "I shan't be begging, I assure you." She looked at her watch. "I must go. Thank you for breakfast."

He stood up when she did. "So you won't meet me."

"No. Thank you for asking, but it's much better not." Lana picked up her bag and left. One block on, she turned to see if he was following.

He was not.

Both relieved and disappointed, Lana continued to her office and thought about Daniel Hunter all the way.

ONCE SHE entered her office building, Lana tried to banish Daniel from her mind. She was here to work and not to daydream over charming, good-looking men she would never see again. And yet the thought of Daniel managed to accompany her up to her floor and into her office. She had been alone for so long, Daniel's attention felt as welcome as the sun peeping through the clouds on a rainy day.

Lana slid her portfolio into the space under her desk. Providing a welcome diversion, her assistant Catharine bumped the door open using a rolling rack of clothing as a battering ram. She pushed the rack into position in front of the desk, where it would be in direct view, and centered the rack precisely against the wall.

She sent a disapproving glance at the bolts of fabric stashed in random corners and the walls where photographs of models, both clothed and in various states of undress, were pinned. Catharine would have lined up every photograph perfectly, using some common denominator known only to her, if Lana had let her.

"Why all these gifts, Catharine? It's not my birthday."

Ignoring her wisecrack, Catharine stopped frowning when she paused to examine Lana's suit with obvious admiration. "Thierry Mugler?"

"And the blouse is Katranzou." Lana gestured at Catharine's flamboyant minidress, patterned with a digital print in peacock blue, green, purple, and minor points of red. "Let me guess. Peter Pilotto around 2010?"

"Vintage. Got it on sale at a secondhand shop, and you know how I love a sale." Catharine pointed at her feet. "What do you think of the shoes?" They were bright red and somehow managed to work with the dress.

"You do like your bright colors." Lana would not have picked those shoes.

"And only someone with a model figure like yours can rock a cropped pant, high heel, and tight little jacket. But we match." Catharine pointed at the swirl of mixed prints on Lana's silk blouse. "Sometimes I wish I were as tall as you."

"But not often." Lana got up and circled her desk to look at the clothing on the rack.

"No, I like when my man is taller than me. Which is lucky seeing as my husband has eight inches on me in altitude." Catharine set a stack of papers on Lana's desk. "I'll e-mail your schedule for today as soon as I get back to my desk. Here are the details on these garments. This is for the shoot next month, by the way. Our creative director and fearless leader Isabelle would like you to do something with…" she squinted at the ceiling and recited, "…Haute Macabre. Whatever that might be."

"You don't have to pretend, Catharine. You know perfectly well what it means."

"Doesn't really matter what it means to me. What does it mean to you? That's more to the point, as you're getting the big bucks for thinking these things up."

"Ooh, well, the first thing I thought of when you mentioned it was an ominous midnight-blue forest with moody shadows and sudden shocks of light. And perhaps antlers made of dead twigs on the models. With white wigs teased up into towering mohawks. And facial jewelry. But who knows, that may change as I cogitate. What else did Isabelle say?"

"She also said on a budget." Catharine squinted at the rack as if trying to picture what Lana described. "But Isabelle always does say that. The budget part, I mean."

"Has she chosen a photographer?"

"Pavlo Marsh."

"Excellent. He'll be able to pull off any concept I come up with and add a few surrealistic touches of his own." Lana slid the garments to one end and started to examine the details of each dress.

"Let me know when you decide on accessories and I'll set up a spreadsheet for each outfit." Catharine rubbed her hands together with anticipation. "And then we go shopping. Très fun!"

"Opulent, isn't it?" Lana indicated a dress of gray-blue satin. Swirls of various-sized beads arranged on the fabric in a flowing pattern reminded her of pebbles gleaming in a brook. She picked up the next dress and turned the hanger to watch the play of light like sunbeams dancing on rippling water. "I'm beginning to sense a water theme here. Borrowing accessories from designers isn't precisely shopping."

"It's cheaper. You get all the fun of shopping without emptying your own bank account and you don't get bored with them in the long run. The hard part is making sure I return everything to the right designer."

"That's the kind of challenge that makes your eyes sparkle. You excel in it, which is why designers are always happy to see your face when I send you out begging."

"Thank you for noticing." Catharine went to the open door and then turned back. "You're looking more cheerful than usual this morning. Don't, or rather *do*, tell me you finally met someone."

Lana held the dress in front of her face to hide a smile. "I did, but it's not what you think. Someone kindly bought me a coffee this morning. However, I shall probably never see him again."

Catharine pounced. "Him? You met a man? Finally!"

"Catharine, don't make me into a project. I know you're hideously organized and once you set your mind to something, nothing can stop you until you achieve your goal. But I know you and your plans, and I don't—" Lana stopped talking because Catharine was laughing.

"Lana, you are *ma petite chou* except on this one subject. I didn't say one word about fixing you up, did I? All I asked was whether you met someone. Don't worry, doll, I don't see you as a project." Catharine went to the door and shut it gently. "It's just that you're so beautiful, and so smart and stylish and funny. I wish you had someone to take care of you."

"I can take care of myself."

"Yes, you and your little friends you call the dwarfs, but I didn't mean you need a caretaker. You love your job, but that's all you do. You stay late, you work weekends—I wish you enjoyed yourself more."

"I do love my work." Lana kept it light even though Catharine hit a sore spot. "So I'll just keep on enjoying that and working with you."

"Work isn't all there is to life. You should—but never mind. I shouldn't tell you what you should do." Catharine opened the door again. "If you take my advice and it turns out wrong, you'll blame me, but I wish you had someone."

Perhaps the chance meeting with Daniel had affected her more than she thought. Lana didn't mean to spill over, but the words burst out spontaneously. "Maybe we don't all get a happy ending, have you ever thought of that? Maybe enjoying my work is as good as it gets. And it's pretty terrific to be going on with. How many people get to do what they love?"

"Absolutely, many people get stuck in jobs they loathe and they don't get their knight in shining armor either. Plus, you're great at what you do. A genius!" Catharine brightened up at that.

Lana laughed. "Sure, I'm a genius."

"I am a glass-half-full girl myself. And at least if you're not dating, he's not cheating on you, so there's a silver lining in every cloud."

Lana laughed, although perhaps she shouldn't have. Clearly Catharine had some feelings about cheating. Whether it happened to her or a friend, Lana didn't feel she could ask when she kept her own personal life out of the office. Cheating had never been a problem for Lana. If one didn't date, one didn't get cheated on. "Thank you, Catharine. We'll look at the world through rose-colored glasses together."

"Except they're pink! I hate pink." With that Catharine left Lana to gain inspiration from the garments on the rack.

Lana picked up another dress, a teal halter from Naeem Khan, with delicate silver beading covering every inch. On a hanger it didn't look like much, but she knew exactly how it would hang on the right model. She had a sudden vision of herself wearing this dress and dancing in Daniel's arms. Hastily she hung up the dress and slammed the door shut on that image. Where had *that* come from? It had been years since she last danced, and then it had been a folk dance at school in gym class. Ridiculous.

Lana had work to do and a deadline to meet. She didn't have time to swan around all day daydreaming about dancing with a man she didn't even know. He'd probably step on her feet anyway.

THAT EVENING, after Lana locked the door to her flat behind her, she took in a deep breath and savored it. The faint hint of coffee and wood floor polish smelled like home. Her flat was the one place she could take off the mask and be at peace, free from expectations. No one ever saw her as she truly was when she retreated here.

Tonight Lana would meet her friends for dinner, but not until later. She had enough time to relax and change before going out to meet them.

Her sanctuary was lovely, everything she'd dreamed of long ago in another country and in another life.

Although the living room was small, Lana had decorated with several shades of ivory and cream to make it feel larger, with an occasional punch of bold color: a turquoise velvet chair, several brilliant red pillows on the couch, and fresh flowers in a glass vase. She bent to inhale the scent of the roses she'd bought for herself.

Ornate iron railings guarded a balcony too small to step out onto, but when the windows were open, the room felt much larger. The late winter air made it too chilly to open them, but the afternoon light streaming in and the view of gray slate rooftops still made her breath catch.

Lana crossed to the window and took her place behind the curtains. The few passersby on the street below were busy with their own concerns and hurried past without glancing up.

Of course Daniel wasn't there. He'd apologized for following her, and Lana believed him, but she was almost disappointed. Since that morning, she'd progressed from the dancing fantasy to passionate kissing despite her best efforts to erase him from her thoughts. In her imagination he was a great kisser. The color of his eyes had reminded her of light shimmering on the ocean. His hands…. But she had to pull herself together. She'd told Daniel to go away and he had. The end of another incident that meant nothing and led nowhere. In the meantime, she had a party to get ready for.

Lana went to the black lacquer table that served as both desk and dining table, and turned on the television set to get the weather report so she could decide what to wear.

She kicked off her shoes and dropped onto the couch to rub her feet. The newscaster droned on about some human-interest story in which Lana had no interest.

The mirror over the fireplace reflected the honeyed light of the setting sun into the room, lulling her into a sensuous awareness of her own body. Lana hadn't permitted herself to think about sex all day, especially with Daniel, but here she sat, once again dreaming about going to bed with a man she barely knew. Far better to think about her outfit for tonight than pine for someone she couldn't have.

The monotone chant of the newscaster must have lulled Lana into a doze, because she awoke with a start to a familiar voice speaking in English. Raising her head from the back of the couch, she darted a glance around the flat in confusion.

The voice was coming from her television.

"…marriage only between a man and a woman. Same-sex couples have no legal right to marry. The Same Sex Couples Act of 2013 has forced the state to recognize this morally repugnant union, and it must be repealed. This law can only lead to the inevitable corruption of our children and the violation of the rights of Christians. What will come next? Marriage between family members, minors, or perhaps even other species?"

The camera cut to the newscaster, who continued in French. "And that was from a speech by Conservative British MP Barrett Reynolds, who continues his crusade to repeal—"

Lana got up and turned the TV off. "Pompous arse," she muttered. She went to close the curtains, but not before she checked the street once more. Daniel still wasn't there. As he said he wouldn't be.

Impatient with herself for continuing to dwell on the forbidden subject, Lana checked her watch. "Better get ready. Fuck, I'm going barmy, talking out loud to myself. Pretty soon I'll acquire a cat or five and become a loony old cat lady."

Lana went to the bedroom and stood before the mirrored doors of her wardrobe. She removed her clothing slowly, putting away each item as soon as she took it off.

When he was naked and Roland again for the moment, he examined his nude body with detachment. Slim and pale, his body was smooth except for the black curls at the root of his cock. Roland twisted his long hair up on top of his head and then let it fall again to brush over his bare shoulders. Roland shivered at the light touch. He could see the beauty of his male self here in the privacy of his room, but he dared not go outside without his disguise. Instead of a ridiculously feminine boy who became a target virtually wherever he went, he could instead present as a beautiful woman with a secret known only to three friends. Roland no longer knew himself whether he was addicted to dressing this way or drawn to the safety the camouflage afforded him, but he was clear on the fact that this was part of who he was.

After he pinned up his hair, Roland went into the bathroom to take a quick shower. Soaping himself all over, he leaned against the wall to give his cock a few gentle strokes. Immediately he was lost in the fantasy of Daniel's hands caressing him. Roland stopped touching himself and leaned against the wall, eyes closed, breathing hard. Abruptly he reached for the faucet and turned off the hot water, flinching as the cold made his cock shrivel. So much for that.

When he tired of shivering, he turned off the water and stepped out. He wrapped himself in a towel and rubbed vigorously. Standing in front of the mirror again, Roland smiled at himself and flicked a quick salute in temporary farewell. Time to become Lana again.

He picked out a bra and matching thong. The delicate silk was cool to the touch but warmed quickly against his skin. Finding consolation in his clothing as usual, Roland admired the sheen of aqua silk against his creamy skin as he modeled the underwear. He rubbed his fingers over the triangular cups until his nipples were taut against the silk, casting little shadows underneath each nub. His cock started to fill the crotch of his thong, but he stopped himself. Not thinking about Daniel. Not yet. Or maybe ever.

Tonight he would have to tell the dwarfs about meeting Daniel.

Roland never should have agreed to that coffee. Daniel was very handsome. So often the good-looking ones, with the careless entitlement that came of being objects of desire themselves, demanded a perfection Roland could never deliver. However, this man seemed more complex. Intriguing. Or maybe Roland was just deluding himself. Daniel was a man.

Deliberately shaking off the memory of their conversation that morning, he continued to dress. Roland pulled on skinny jeans and a fitted black top with rhinestone clips, and big, floofy sleeves. He held on to the wardrobe to slip into black suede boots embroidered in scarlet, knowing Colin at least would appreciate them. He sat down at the dressing table to apply makeup. His skin was so smooth he needed no foundation, but he painted on eye shadow, liner, and mascara with care. Roland brushed his brows into flawless arches and then leaned forward to apply lipstick. After finishing off with a dusting of powder, she examined her face and smiled. Roland had disappeared and Lana looked back from the mirror again.

She went to the wardrobe for a leather jacket. She twisted from side to side in front of the mirror to check her silhouette from every angle before giving a nod of approval. Once dressed, and with her tall, slender figure, Lana looked much like any model in Paris. Flat-chested, but so many models were. Walking a runway would have been her ultimate dream, but to her regret, she'd never had the courage to try it. And now, with her hard-won confidence, Lana was too old at twenty-seven to start.

Lana picked up a leather satchel and slung it over her shoulder. She turned out the lights as she went through the flat. She hesitated inside the door and braced herself to face the world again. And even worse, the dwarfs. Lana couldn't imagine they would exactly welcome her news.

CHAPTER 4

"SO WHERE'S your girlfriend tonight, Col?" Dominick looked up from setting the table, a task he performed at their monthly dinners at Colin's insistence.

Colin darted a sharp glance at the table to inspect Dom's work. "Forks on the left. Simone is having a girls' night out with her friends."

"And you're having a boys' night in with yours." Dom chortled when Colin's face flushed red. "Égalité. Give her my very best regards and tell her we missed her."

Colin dropped a pile of napkins onto the table. "Fold those up nicely, will you, Dom?"

"Nicely. What qualifies as nicely?" Dom sighed and picked them up.

"Make them look good as opposed to merely flinging them in the general direction of the table." At the sound of the doorbell, Colin raised his brows and smirked. "Want to make a small wager on who it is?"

"Find another sucker. Not wasting my money. You know it's Terry." Relieved at the interruption, Dom started for the door, napkins still in hand. Colin was far too particular about place settings that would last only minutes until everyone sat down. The best he could do would be to fold the napkins in half. Then Colin would probably demand he origami the napkins into peacocks or some such silliness.

"True, Lana's always late. Prerogative of being a girl." Colin disappeared back into the kitchen.

Before Dom had the door open wide enough to see who was standing there, he spoke. "Terry, we were expecting you."

"Ha-ha, Lana's late as usual?" Terry gave Dom the obligatory handshake/man-hug combo. "How is Colin and the beauteous Simone?"

"Colin is busy whipping up a masterpiece in the kitchen and Simone is out for the evening. And your lady love?"

"Martine is doing quite well, thank you. Sent her best." Terry took off his coat and hung it on the rack by the door. "She's visiting her mum tonight. Good thing we had this dinner already arranged or I'd've had to go along."

Colin emerged from the kitchen, and held out a bottle and corkscrew. "Make yourself useful. Open that wine and let it breathe."

"Terry's turn. I've been useful enough already." Dom put his hands behind his back to hide the unfolded napkins.

"Slacker." Terry took off his glasses to read the label. "You're wasting a fine old Médoc on us?"

"Put a sock in it or I might serve a recorked Chardonnay instead." Colin bustled back into the kitchen.

"White wine with beef?" Terry called out.

"Quelle horreur." Dom grinned. "Better not let the culinary police get wind of that."

"You mean a sommelier, and the rules have changed, you morons. Matching wines to food by color is completely old hat, although I'm rather impressed you were able to identify the protein by scent, Ter." Colin stood in the doorway, staring at his watch. "Haven't you finished with those napkins yet, Dom? The first course is approaching the apex of perfection." He hurried back into the kitchen.

"Lana can do it when she arrives. You know she's better than me at that shit," Dom said. "I may be a bender, but I'm not artsy-fartsy."

"A clear traitor to your kind." Terry eased the cork out of the bottle.

The bell rang again and Dom hurried to the door. "Well, if it isn't Miss Lana. How are you?"

Lana stooped to kiss both Dom's cheeks and give him a hug. "Quite well, thank you, Happy. And you?"

"Aw, quit with the dwarf names already, Snow White."

"Not a chance." She patted his head and he ducked away from her.

Dish towel in hand, Colin came out of the kitchen to greet her. "Finally! You look beautiful, as usual, Lana. Now sit so we can eat."

"Thank you ever so, Bashful."

"Oh, quit rubbing it in that you're taller than us with that dwarf shit." Colin wrapped his arms around Lana. "Do you always have to wear heels?"

"Certainement. I knew you'd love them." When he released her, Lana turned her foot to show the heel of her boot. "I wore the short ones tonight. These are only three inches!"

"Girls *are* allowed to wear flats, you know," Terry called from the dining room.

"I'd still be taller than any of you runts," Lana responded immediately.

"May I take your wrap?"

"You're such a gentleman, Col." Lana set her bag on a chair and shrugged herself out of the jacket.

"He's just hurrying you along so the dinner isn't ruined." Dom winked at Lana.

"We would have started without you," Colin said.

"Try it on someone else," Dom jeered.

Terry put his glasses back on to watch Lana fluff out her voluminous organza sleeves. "You sure wouldn't want to wear that picking apples, Snow White. You might get snagged on a branch."

"Of course I wouldn't. I'd wear my apple-picking ensemble instead." Lana held both arms out and turned in a slow circle for them.

"Note the juxtaposition of volume between the full sleeve and the close-fitting silhouette of the body."

"Aren't you afraid you're going to drag those sleeves through your plate?" Dom made a face, but damn. Lana knew how to work a look that would be ridiculous on anyone else. "You only came to show off your outfit, didn't you?"

"This top is both interesting and *dramatic*." Lana waved her arms to let the fabric fall into graceful folds. "And yes, I do enjoy the chance to show off my ensembles to *someone*, even if you trogs don't appreciate it."

Terry came forward to receive his kisses and a hug. "How do you balance on those stilts again?"

"I walk better in heels, you know that."

"Yeah, you always were a klutz." Dom looked around at his friends. They were all average height, and Lana did tower over them in her stocking feet. The extra height of her heels added insult to injury, but Dom couldn't help smiling up at her before he chucked his cache of linen napkins into her hands. "Here, you're good at making things look pretty. Fold these up or Colin will boycott and we'll get no dessert."

"I think we'd better sit down before Colin starts beating us with a wooden spoon. We wouldn't want his sauce to break-dance or something equally dire," Terry said.

Colin poked his head into the dining room. "It's entirely up to you. You can savor the results of my genius now or choke down the dry, unappetizing remnants later as long as you're fully aware that it would be thoroughly your own fault."

"I vote for savoring Colin's genius." After folding the napkins and placing them at each setting, Lana stood back to judge the effect. "Can we eat now? I'm starving."

"Now you're all showing a tiny bit of common sense. I'll bring out the first course." Colin disappeared back into the kitchen. He came back in, proudly bearing a tray. "You're probably wondering why I asked you all here tonight—"

"Colin!" Lana's voice was drowned out by Dom and Terry's louder tones as they all said his name in unison. "Not again."

TERRY GROANED with satisfaction after dessert was only a faint memory and coffee was served. "Lana, you can really pack it away."

"Are both legs hollow or only the one? Your stomach's as flat as a board." Colin patted his own comfortably. "You're still as skinny as you ever were."

"Skinny? *Slender* sounds romantic. *Slim* I could live with. But *skinny*? Especially when I eat barely enough to keep up my slender, girlish figure." Lana winced at the artificial timbre of her laughter and hoped they couldn't tell how nervous she was. Waffling about whether to tell them about Daniel, Lana kept waiting for a convenient opening in the conversation that never came. She couldn't blurt it out apropos of nothing.

Dom held his glass up to the light and then took a sip of his liqueur. "You're a great cook, Col. Seriously. You learned your trade well."

"That's a bit like me saying you're an excellent typist rather than an award-winning reporter. I did come to Paris to hone my culinary skills, remember?"

"It wasn't much of an award. Not like a Pulitzer. And yes, I do remember. Best idea you ever had. So the dinner parties are turning out a success?" Dom asked.

"Don't bother acknowledging the compliment. Let me show you how it's done." Colin patted his own back. "Thanks, Colin, for noticing even that minor award!"

"You know Dom can't stop with the questions." Terry's eyes twinkled.

"I can always use the publicity if you're willing to puff me up." Colin grabbed the wine bottle and held it to his mouth like a microphone. "When I first had the idea of hosting dinner parties at home instead of cooking in a restaurant, Simone was a bit concerned as to where we would find customers, but almost from the start it's

40

been a success. People seem to prefer the more intimate setting and the chance to ask questions."

"Do you really enjoy letting strangers into your home every night?" Lana shuddered at the thought. Except for Dom, even the dwarfs rarely came to her place.

Colin nodded energetically. "We thrive on it! Love meeting new people and having a chat with them while I'm sharing what I love to do. I actually get a bit dull and lethargic if I go too long without interacting with people."

"Oh, shut up. You, dull and lethargic?" Complacently, Terry looked around the room as if he owned it. "This place was rather a find. Not many flats about with a modern kitchen. Good thing you rate as a friend, because if I'd listed it publicly, it would have been snapped up before you even saw it."

"I said I was grateful," Colin said. "That's why I don't charge you for these expensive soirées."

"And here I thought it was because you loved us." Lana pouted.

"Maybe I do, just a bit." Colin grinned. "A toast to true friends who stick by you, in good times and bad. I can't imagine my life without you guys."

Terry held up his glass. "All for one and one for all."

Lana groaned. "Not the Three Musketeers toast again."

"What's wrong with it?" Dom demanded. "You get to be the token girl."

"Constance Bonacieux." Terry's French accent was impeccable.

"I loved the costuming." Lana fluffed her voluminous sleeves. "But Constance dies at the end. That's why I'd rather play at Snow White and the Seven Dwarfs."

"Except we're average height," Colin pointed out.

Always the peacekeeper, Terry changed the subject. "What about you, Dom? Any nice boys in your future?"

Lana noticed the quick glance Dom shot her before he answered, and when he did, she understood the reason for his caution.

"Yes, as a matter of fact, I have finally met someone rather interesting. Another reporter at the paper, Gilles Martin."

41

"Tell us more." Lana rested her chin on her hand to hide how hard the news hit her. Because he was also single, she saw more of Dom than the other two. A new boyfriend meant he would be too busy for her. As if she needed even more reminders of her lonely single state. However, she didn't want her envy to spoil Dom's happiness. "What's this Gilles like to look at?"

"He's pretty good-looking, if I do say so." Dom smiled bashfully. "I think he modeled a bit when he was younger. But it's not about his looks. Gilles is smart and funny, and best of all, he likes me too."

"So we've all—" Colin stopped abruptly and eyed Lana anxiously.

"Found someone. Except me." Lana finished for him.

Discomfort written all over his face, Terry snagged the bottle and poured more wine into Lana's glass. "This is a bit awkward, Lana, but I always sort of expected you and Dom to get together at some point. You both like boys so, uh…."

Lana fluttered her eyelashes at Dom when he looked at her, and they both giggled. "Actually, we did go on a date once."

"It wasn't what you think, though," Dom added hastily.

Terry belted out a dirty laugh.

"Get your mind out of the gutter," Dom growled.

Lana jerked her thumb at Dom. "Hotshot reporter here needed a cover date for the holiday party. Remember when he was working for that filthy tabloid in London? He didn't want to end up on the front cover as a headline on a day they were running short on scandal."

Colin exploded with laughter. "So he took *you*? A gay man took a boy dressed up as a girl as a cover date so his coworkers would think he was straight? If that isn't the definition of irony."

"Hey, it was an emergency." Dom grinned. "And she's hot. I was the envy of the party. Half the guys were coming on to her, and their dates were furious."

"But I was true to Dom the entire evening, even though he stepped on my foot repeatedly when we were dancing."

"I didn't hurt you, just scuffed up your old shoe a bit."

Lana frowned in mock anger. "They weren't old, and I liked those shoes."

"So it didn't work out, huh?" Terry asked.

"I like boys who look like boys." Dom glanced at Lana in apology. "Even though you're quite stunning, Lana. Hell, your legs should be registered as a national landmark."

"Thank you for that lovely compliment, Happy." Lana put her fingers to her throat and tugged gently at her scarf. "And I would like boys who like boys who prefer to dress like girls. Not that I've ever found one of those mythical creatures."

Terry furrowed his forehead. "Never say never."

Dom reached out to nudge her arm. "Don't give up hope, Lana. There has to be one somewhere. Remember, Snow White gets the prince at the end."

"Oh, that's like looking for a unicorn in a rainbow forest." She managed to force a smile. This was the perfect opportunity, and if she didn't say it now... she lifted her glass and took a gulp to fortify herself.

But apparently Colin wasn't on the same wavelength. "So I know we've never discussed this before, but what is it you call yourself?"

"Lana, you idiot." Lana rolled her eyes. "Duh."

"No, I meant, um, transgender, cross-dresser, gender-fluid—what?"

She startled them all by slamming her hand down on the table and the liqueur glasses rang out Lana's anger. "What difference does it make? Why do I need a label?"

Terry stared at her, his eyes wide with fear and his mouth hanging open. She almost could have laughed at his expression. Almost, but this was too much.

But Colin went on bravely. "I'm sorry, babe. I'm not asking to piss you off. I didn't really think too much about you wearing girls' clothes when we met. We were kids. Not like any of us knew anything about sex back then anyway. But it seems like wearing these clothes has just made things harder for you."

"And you have nothing but the clothes," Dom pointed out. "No boyfriend. No girlfriend you can confide in."

43

"I have a job I love and I live as I like without anyone forcing me to be something I'm not!" Lana tried to keep her cool. These were her friends.

"No one's saying you should change. I just want to know—"

"And how is having a label going to change a damn thing?" Lana cut Colin off. After all this time and from her friends, no less! "You claim to like me as I am, so what possible difference does it make whatever I choose to call myself?"

"No, Lana, I *love* you as you are, and I always will, no matter what. I just want to understand, but if this is too uncomfortable...." Colin shrugged. "So be it."

"Why've you never asked about this before?"

Colin flushed red and averted his gaze, staring at the empty cup in front of him. "This is far more uncomfortable than I thought it would be. Because I'm so used to you I never really wondered before."

Lana counted to ten for patience. "Fair enough. I'll try to explain, although the why of it is a mystery to me too. As far back as I can remember, I loved feminine clothing. All the colors and fabrics! Ruffles even, although I was three then and wouldn't be caught dead in them now. I was always so jealous of my sister's clothes, I used to sneak into her closet to visit with them. They were so much prettier than the rubbish they made boys wear. I thought if I could wear dresses like hers, I would feel... pretty." Lana smiled. "And I did too. Until my parents caught me."

"I'm sure your parents didn't appreciate that," Dom said.

"You're not wrong about that." Lana shuddered at the memory. She'd never shared the entire story of her home life with them, and she wouldn't now. Tedious and boring, and they already pitied her enough. "I saw my father on the telly tonight. Still out spouting hate about gays. Imagine how he'd feel to see me now."

Dom's brows snapped together. "MP Barrett Reynolds is an asshole. I saw that interview."

"They tried to 'toughen me up.' As if it's a criminal offense to dress in women's clothing. Worse than committing murder."

"People are weird about sex," Terry blurted.

44

"Profound, Ter." Dom rolled his eyes heavenward. "But don't I know it. Just being queer is no walk in the park either."

"I'm sorry." Colin drooped in misery. "I used to think if it bothered so many people, maybe you just shouldn't do it, but dressing in girls' clothing is pretty harmless. And who am I to tell you what to do—shit, I never should've brought this up."

"But since you have, let me be clear with you, I don't feel I was born in the wrong body. I like myself just fine. I don't *want* to live a lie, but when I go out dressed like this, no one stares or throws a fit because I'm effeminate and wrong. I feel free, like I can be myself. I feel… safe." Except that wasn't strictly true either. Her feelings of safety seemed to run from one end of the continuum to the other. Lana wanted to be left alone, but then someone like Daniel would come along and she wanted what she couldn't have.

The seconds stretched into minutes as her friends sat in silence, watching her. Although Lana felt their sympathy, her frustration took over again. "And now you want a label? It is exhausting to have to explain and define myself. Well, tough shit. I refuse to be compartmentalized. You want to know what I am? I'm a boy who likes being a boy—but who also likes to look pretty. I enjoy putting on makeup, doing my hair, and wearing beautiful dresses. I love knowing that I look fantastic when I walk out my front door. So categorize *that*!"

Dom stood and applauded. "Bravo! Lay down the law, girl."

Having gotten that out of her system, Lana relaxed into a smile and leaned back in her chair. "Perhaps a bit too ranty?"

"Maybe just a little over the top." Dom grinned back at her and sat down. "I mean, we *are* your friends, remember? We're supposed to pick on you. Keep you on your toes."

"I'm sorry, Lana." Colin looked and sounded awkward but persisted. "Sorry about the compartment bit. It's just that speaking about dating as we were, I merely wondered if you'd ever gone onto the Internet to, um, I mean, to each his own and all that, but what with all the sexual freedom about, I figured there must be some sort of dating service for people like you. Where you could be up-front about who you are. Right from the start."

She stared at him in surprise. "Darling Bashful. Have you been fishing about online trying to find me a date?"

Colin gulped audibly. "Well, I did just think to have a look, but then I got confused. I didn't know which box you would prefer to fill in for, ahem, what you are. Because I care about you and I don't want you to be alone and I thought I could, like, help."

"That's really rather sweet. Now I feel rather remorseful for getting a bit ratty with you." Lana tapped her fingers on the table. "I have been to those sites, and they're not for me."

"But why?" Terry cut in. "We all have someone and you're alone. Don't you want to at least try?"

"I might as well shoot off the other barrel now. Those sites fetishize people like me. They turn us into a kink. Men who go to those sites are looking for an object to use to fulfill their fantasies, not a real person." A quaver shook her voice. "I've been on some of those sites. It's all men asking what are you wearing underneath, not who you are."

"Is that so bad? At least you'd get some action."

"Fucking hell, Terry! Don't be tacky!"

Lana grabbed Dom's clenched fist. "It's all right, Dom. Calm down." She turned to Terry. "This isn't a sexual fetish for me. Me going on a date? Before I would dare accept an invitation, I would have to endure a very uncomfortable conversation, and believe me when I say it would be uncomfortable."

"Maybe you're better off alone." Terry turned his wineglass in his fingers without looking at her. "Some people are."

This time Colin's eyes blazed with anger. "Terry! What a rotten thing to say. That's like telling her to give up altogether."

"Sorry, I didn't mean that Lana has become the patron saint of lost causes." Terry finally looked her straight in the face. "I only meant you might be… safer."

"I'm all right, really." Lana picked up her liqueur glass and emptied it in one swallow to muster up some courage. She braced herself. "Besides, just today a man followed me for at least a block, so I must not be completely devoid of attraction."

Immediately Dom leaned forward, intent on getting answers. "Was it that same guy who followed you before? Did he talk to you?"

Now or never. Lana sucked in a deep breath. "It wasn't as much following as accompanying. He was waiting for me near Henri's and asked if he could join me. We had a delightful breakfast together."

Struck dumb, her friends all stared at her with their mouths open.

Finally Dom spoke. "Are you completely out of your mind, Rolly?"

"Don't be such a dick, Dom, and the name's Lana." Now that the news was out, she could breathe again. She refilled her glass.

"I'm not a dick!" Dom sputtered. "I'm just—"

"Look up *dick* in Urban Dictionary, because your picture's posted there," Terry interrupted.

"If it is, I know who posted it!" Dom shot back.

"Crabby," Colin offered.

"A know-it-all mother hen," Lana joined in.

"Control freak," Terry said.

"Bossy." Colin cackled.

"Obstreperous."

Dom raised his brows. "Learn a new word this week, Terry?"

Terry shrugged. "Martine and I were playing Scrabble, dickwad. You're also supercilious, pushy, and a complete and utter prat."

"Terry, you really must learn to be more direct," Dom said. "And if I'm so fucking awful, why do you guys even want to hang around with me?"

"Who said we want to?" Terry sniggered at his own repartee.

Lana wrapped her arms around Dom in a hug and gave him a smack on the cheek, leaving a lipstick kiss on his face. "Because you're *our* arrogant dickwad prat and we wouldn't have you any other way, Dommy-wommy."

"Get off." Dom tried to push Lana away, but he was grinning. "You keep up the baby talk and you'll have me barfing from sugar overload."

"And put my dinner to waste," Colin added.

"Have it your way." Lana let go of him and waited for the barrage of questions she knew was still coming.

Dom rubbed at his cheek to remove Lana's lip print. "I'm trying not to be a dick—"

"Try harder." Colin clinked his glass against Terry's and they both laughed.

"I'm only a bit protective," Dom insisted. "It's only because I care about you."

"A bit?" Lana patted his hand to soothe him. "I know you are, but you really need to stop flinging orders at me. 'Don't talk to him! Don't go to the café!' I can take care of myself."

Dom studied her face and then he spoke more quietly. "I'm afraid for you."

"I know you are. And I appreciate that and everything else you've done for me." Lana squeezed his hand. "You three are the most important people in my life. You know me, the real me."

"But this stalker guy doesn't." Colin tapped the table with a forefinger. "Who the hell is he?"

"His name is Daniel Hunter." Lana took another swallow to prepare for the interrogation. "He invited me out to dinner—"

"I hope you said no!" Lana jumped when Dom smacked the table louder than she had earlier. "You'd better not meet him."

Colin eyed his glassware uneasily.

"I said no, all right?" Lana raised both hands and pressed them to her mouth to keep from exploding again. "I told him no." No matter how much she wanted to say yes.

Dominick stared at her. "I bet you wanted to say yes."

"So what if I did?" Lana grimaced. "I can't do both. I can keep my little secret to myself or risk everything for one solitary date that would probably turn out a complete disaster anyway."

"Not such a little secret. If he found out—" Colin stopped abruptly.

"I know, I know," Lana said.

"So you're saying there's no way out for you," Terry said.

"I'm open if you have any brilliant ideas." Lana smiled, but it was a pathetic effort and she knew it. She hated them feeling sorry for her. "Except that site online Colin found."

"Really the only way I see is for you to be up-front, Lana. This isn't the kind of secret you can spring on a guy on the second date," Colin said.

"But if the first date is a fiasco, there's no need for me to explain anything at all because there'll never be a second," Lana argued.

Terry gestured at her outfit. "Are the clothes worth living alone for the rest of your life? You could live out and still work in fashion. Lord knows there's enough gay men in the field, and gay marriage is legal here and in the UK."

Even though they accepted her as she was, she couldn't explain her need to dress like a woman to their satisfaction. That need wasn't logical, it was emotional. Try as they might, they would never truly get it, which made their unwavering support doubly precious. "It's not just about the clothes. It runs deeper than that. It would have been agony working with beautiful clothes and not getting to wear them, but I could have tried them on in private if that was all there was to it."

"And you look damned good in them too. You haven't changed much since we were kids, other than the makeup and clothing. I've always thought you blend the best of feminine and masculine, but perhaps it's just because you're so damn pretty." Terry stared at her face in fascination. "Androgyny could have been your middle name."

"Roland Androgyny Reynolds. No, doesn't work. Terrible name for a girl." Lana attempted a smile even though she felt rotten. Knowing she had to forget Daniel and undergoing Colin's clumsy interrogation was too much for one day.

"Or a boy."

"I am Lana Renault. It has a ring, doesn't it?" Her forced smile slipped away. "Maybe I'll never find love, but I won't change for any man. This is the me I want to be. Either he takes me as I am or I walk."

"You go, girl! And if he doesn't accept you as you are, he's not a real man anyway." Dom gave a sharp nod of approval.

"Who?" Terry asked in a stage whisper.

"The hypothetical man Lana's not dating," Colin whispered back.

Lana giggled at their attempt to cheer her up. "Besides, I am a glass-half-full girl. I'm not completely alone. At least I have you guys." Lana reached out to grab Dom's and Terry's hands.

"And we love you just as you are." Colin leaned across the table to pat her arm, making her sleeve flutter.

"Always have." Terry nodded.

"I know you do, and I can't express what a comfort it is." Lana let go of her friends and raised her glass. "I live in Paris. I have a fabulous job in fashion and you three. I don't need a man to be happy. To our friendship, my dwarfy brothers. However much you all drive me to the brink at times, I hope nothing ever comes between us for the rest of our lives."

Terry grinned. "*You're* driven to the brink? What about us? You're never on time—"

"You can't cook," Colin interjected.

"Oh, pile it on. Besides, I don't have to cook as long as you're willing to feed me." Lana gave Colin a hopeful smile. "You may have noticed the size of my bag, Colin dearest. And it's empty."

"I'll fill it before you leave, love," Colin promised.

Dom leaned forward to grab her hand. "We're not just friends, Lana, we're family."

As Lana laced her fingers with his, she looked at each of her friends in turn. "To friends who mean more to me than family."

"To friends forever."

Solemnly, they raised their glasses and clinked before they drank their toast.

Dom put his glass down and belched.

"Charming."

Dom grinned. "And now while you're filling Lana's bag, I'd better call for a taxi. I'm going to make sure you get home all right."

"I can get home on my own just fine."

"You drank more wine than you usually do and I'm seeing you safely home." Dom burped again.

"Who's to see you home, then?"

"I'll trust the taxi driver to slow down and push me out." Dom grinned and poured more wine into his glass.

Amused, Lana shook her head. "You're tipsy."

Dom clinked his glass against hers. "Takes one to know one."

WHEN SHE returned home from the evening with her friends, the silence of the flat pressed in on Lana. The disclosure about Dom's new boyfriend and then the uncomfortable discussion at dinner made her think. As much as Lana enjoyed working with Catharine, she couldn't really claim their friendship was real when Catharine didn't know the most basic fact of her existence. Lana knew her well enough to know her secret wouldn't make a difference. If Catharine found out, she would never reveal it, but Lana had gotten this far by keeping her identity under her skirt.

And until Lana found a graceful way to reveal it, she couldn't date anyone. The best response she'd ever received was from the man who simply told her he couldn't handle it and walked away. That rejection had hurt enough. Far safer to remain alone with only three real friends to her name.

Which left Lana doomed to have sex only with herself. Reminding herself to look on the bright side, she had to giggle. At least she knew how to have fun with herself.

How nice it would have been to come home to someone and have them put down their book and ask, "Have a nice time with your friends?" After listening to Colin and Terry talk about their girlfriends, Lana felt very alone. Their relationships were "normal," casually accepted by everyone who saw them. Although gay, even Dom had it easier, and hearing him talk about getting to know a new man while Lana had… nothing….

Except her job. She still had to go to work tomorrow. Resigned to the inevitable, Lana began her evening routine. After removing her makeup and getting undressed, she greeted Roland in the mirror again. Then he slipped into a silky nightgown and turned out the lights.

Once in bed, he couldn't resist temptation any longer. All day Roland had tried to stop thinking about the obvious admiration in Daniel's eyes. Each time Roland's thoughts strayed, he'd stopped himself. But now alone in his flat, Roland gave himself the luxury of letting go and exploring the fantasy.

Roland imagined Daniel undressing him and slipped off the nightgown.

Usually masturbating was only about getting off, and he would finish himself off quickly, but not tonight. The blazing heat of his own cock surprised him when he closed his hand around it. He touched himself slowly to build anticipation.

Up and down, with a little swipe of his thumb over the head to spread the fluid leaking from the slit. He saw Daniel naked and the hotness of the image made his hips start to move. He moaned Daniel's name aloud, surprised as the sound escaped him. Roland reached for his balls and cupped them. His cock was lengthening, getting harder and thicker.

Rolling onto his side, Roland reached into the drawer of his side table for a bottle. He flicked the top open and slicked up both hands as he lay back and spread his legs. Now Daniel was kissing him.

With no weight bearing down on him, his hips thrust up in the air. Imagining Daniel licking and biting his nipples, Roland pinched them in turn until they were hard little peaks.

He flipped over onto his stomach, humping the mattress, thrusting his cock into the circle of his thumb and fingers. Daniel had somehow taken residence in his imagination, and Roland wanted to share himself with *someone*. Thrusting into his fist, he spread his legs wide and reached back to tease his hole with the other hand.

In the fantasy, Daniel was talking to him now. Tantalizing Roland by telling him everything he was going to do to him. He circled his hole, quivering with the anticipation as imaginary Daniel said, "I'm going to make you come real soon. I'm going to open up that hole and fuck you real good, baby. That's right, get ready for me."

Roland pushed his finger inside, pretending it was Daniel's cock sliding into him. He pumped his cock faster and faster. When he came, his mouth was open in a silent cry of pleasure and the only sound was his heavy breathing as he panted for air.

CHAPTER 5

WITH NO recent Daniel sightings, Lana judged it safe to return to Henri's. She went back to the usual route to work and stopped at the café to get her morning coffee. To be on the safe side, she peered through the window before she entered. No sign of Daniel, outside or in.

Filled with mingled relief and resignation, Lana took her usual seat at the counter this time. "Bonjour, Henri. Un express, s'il te plaît."

"Bonjour, Lana." Henri continued in French. "May I tempt you with a tart this morning?" He indicated the display of luscious pastries under glass. "Something to cheer you up?"

"Do I look in need of cheering up?" Lana surveyed the choices. "An apple tart, please." She selected a bill from her wallet and laid it on the counter.

But Henri waved it away when he returned with her coffee and tart. "Put that away. Your breakfast has been taken care of for at least a month. That handsome gentleman you met for coffee the other day paid in advance. He left this for you." Henri opened the cash register and searched under the bill tray before pulling out a business card. He winked at Lana when he handed it over. "It's good to see you with a boyfriend at last. A pretty girl like you shouldn't be always alone. The men of Paris must be blind or crazy."

"Merci, Henri." Lana sighed. Him too. She didn't touch the card until her coffee was gone and the tart only a sweet memory. Then she picked up the card and glanced at it. The glossy side showed a painting of a beautiful woman. In her hand, the woman held a white lily, the throat delicately tinged with pink. The contours of her face were painted with precision, while her dress was rendered with quick, impressionistic daubs of cool and warm tones to indicate the folds of her dress. The edges of the garment blurred into the background, making her face the focal point. Lana knew enough about painting to recognize the rigorous technique behind the fluidity of the brush strokes.

She turned the card over. Daniel's name and website were printed there. Underneath he'd written by hand: *In case you ever change your mind....*

Lana was about to rip the card in half but caught Henri sneaking a peek at her in the mirror behind the counter. He'd always been friendly to her, and she didn't want to ruin his chance to play Cupid. Instead she dropped the card into her bag. "The tart was delicious, Henri."

"Merci, Lana. You should call him. M. Hunter looked smitten to me."

"We'll see." Great. She barely managed not to snap at Henri, who'd been nothing but kind to her. But it was so fucking complicated when she couldn't tell people to back off on the dating thing without telling them the *reason*.

All the way to work, Lana kept her eyes open but saw no sign of Daniel. She was glad of that. At least that's what she told herself. He was keeping his word even though he'd found a way to tell her he was still interested. Knowing he was interested gratified Lana but made it all the more difficult to forget him. And after the discussion with the dwarfs last night, forgetting Daniel was the best thing she could do.

DANIEL WAITED until Thursday before going back to Henri's, and he made sure to visit at a time when Lana should be safely at work. He was getting desperate. He couldn't paint and he couldn't get Lana off his mind. Despite the fact he said he would do it, Daniel really didn't want to eat worms, even though he had no doubt the talented chefs of Paris could make him eat them and like it.

On the pavement outside, he checked out the place before going in. The coast was clear. He went to the counter and ordered a coffee.

The café was virtually empty at this hour, so when Henri brought the coffee, he remained to chat. First he gave Daniel a knowing smile and a nod. Then he started the conversation in English. "I gave Lana your card."

"Thank you." Daniel took a sip of his coffee, but he had a feeling acting casual wasn't going to fool Henri. "What did she do?"

Henri shrugged. "She said merci. Put your card in her bag and left."

Disappointed, Daniel nodded to himself. "Well, thanks anyway." He wanted to grill Henri and ask how she looked, how she reacted to receiving his card and if Henri knew Lana's last name, but that would put him right back into stalker territory. Besides, Henri most likely wouldn't tell him a thing anyway.

After finishing his coffee, Daniel left a generous tip. Aimlessly, he started to walk, his hobby of people watching completely forgotten. He jammed his hands into his pockets and stared at the pavement.

He wanted to court Lana. An old-fashioned concept. Since when had he ever taken the time to really get to know a woman? But he wanted to spend time with her and savor every revelation until he'd painted a picture of who she was. Because he didn't know Lana's last name, it would be a bit difficult to pull off the kinds of things one did when courting. Can't send flowers without knowing where to send them.

From their single conversation, he understood she'd been badly hurt at some time. She'd been cautious when he approached her, and if they hadn't been in a public place, she might have run. She'd relaxed a bit while they had coffee, although she never gave him her last name. From the way she laughed, Daniel could tell that Lana liked him.

Everything was going along well until the shattering of that damn plate sliced through the air. Startled by the sudden noise himself, Daniel had still managed to notice her alarms going off. Lana had slammed the doors shut right after Henri broke the plate, and Daniel had been too distracted himself to make a good comeback.

Ever since he'd first seen her, Lana had entered his dreams and taken them over. First it was a wet dream. He really couldn't be held responsible for that, could he? But that progressed to taking fleeting glimpses of her and piecing them together into a dream of what he wanted to happen.

Daniel had to give this one more try. Maybe he could get her to reconsider. If not, he would probably have to leave Paris to flee from temptation. Having run from unwelcome attention himself, he didn't want to be the source of that discomfort to her.

How could he earn another chance with Lana? If he showed up at Henri's unexpectedly, she would never trust him again, and with good reason.

The only solution was to get someone to intercede for him. Daniel drew a few surprised stares when he laughed out loud on the street at the idea of approaching one of the dwarfs to run interference for him. He couldn't remember if Lana had mentioned their actual names, but he was pretty sure Happy would take a lot of pleasure in shutting him down if he suggested such a thing. If Happy even bothered to listen to him. Daniel had a feeling he'd end up with a mouthful of fist if he dared approach Happy.

The only other person he could think of was Henri. How many cups was that today already? But in a good cause, Daniel could sacrifice his nerves. "Always time for another cup of coffee."

Daniel reversed course and retraced his steps, wondering how he could get Henri on his side. Henri had already done him a solid by agreeing to give his card to Lana, but that required no judgment call from Henri. Not quite the same thing as urging Lana to go out with him.

Before he pushed the café door open again, Daniel took in a few slow breaths to steady himself. All the scheming and planning he used to do to get into a woman's pocket, and now he could think of nothing better than the truth. Almost embarrassing.

"Bonjour—" Henri looked up in surprise. "M. Hunter. I know my coffee is good, but is it so difficult to resist you come back twenty minutes after the last cup?"

"Yes, and call me Daniel." Grinning, Daniel took a seat at the counter. "Your coffee is just that good."

"Perhaps this time I could tempt you with a tart?"

"Almond, please." Daniel gave Henri his most charming smile. "As I walked away, a sudden thought occurred to me and I decided I had to ask you. Are you a romantic, Henri?"

"BUT LANA, you would make such a beautiful couple. Men and women were not put on this earth to live alone."

Lana blinked at Henri's impassioned approach but bit back a snappy retort. Based on results, some of them were. The ones with secrets to guard. "I don't—"

"Why can't you give this man a chance? I know you've been hurt, but we all have. It's a part of life, part of the game of love. Nature is kind and those wounds heal. Day by day, they hurt less. You have come to my shop now for five years, and always alone."

"You've seen me with my friends, and they're—"

"Not for you, Lana. Those little men are your comrades, not a lover for you." Firmly, Henri dismissed the dwarfs. "Now this man Daniel, he is interested and he is trying very hard to see you. Does he come and hang around here waiting for you? No. He comes only when you are working and asks me to talk to you. Give him a chance."

"But I don't know—"

"If you never talk to him, how can you get to know him?"

She had never seen Henri so animated. This matchmaking fervor was new to her. Henri stopped to take a swallow of his own coffee and she managed a complete sentence. "Why should I have to get to know him if I don't want to?"

"What, your social calendar is so full you can't fit him in? No, Lana. You are alone for five years now." Henri put his hand on his chest. "Lana, I am thirty years older than you, at least. How long have you known me?"

"Five years, like you said. But—"

"In that time, have I ever lied to you?"

"No, but we haven't—"

"I've gotten to know Daniel over the past two months. He is sophisticated and interesting. Intelligent. He knows how to treat a woman. Having a business like mine, I see many people every day. Some are nice, some not so nice. Daniel is a nice man. What would it hurt to go on one date with him? Right here, with me standing guard to keep you safe." Henri gave her an arch look. "He is a romantic. Like me."

"Would you trust your daughter with Daniel?"

Pausing a moment to consider before he answered, Henri nodded. "I would. He carries secrets just like you and me, but I believe whatever truly bad deeds he has committed are behind him now." Henri's eyes twinkled. "Not that he is a saint. I imagine he is a very accomplished sinner in some ways that a woman would appreciate. He's a handsome man. When other women see you together, they will envy you."

Her cheeks burning, Lana wished she could fan herself, but she wouldn't give Henri the satisfaction. He was enjoying her blush, but at least he thought it was caused by a different sort of embarrassment and not because he'd unwittingly put his finger right on the root of her problem. "I'm sure that—"

"And last time you met, you laughed together. That is very important in a marriage. You seemed to enjoy his company that first day, and he is very handsome."

"Marriage?" Lana couldn't help laughing at Henri's leap from one date to a wedding. "Who said anything about marriage?"

With a sly smile, Henri pushed another of Daniel's cards toward her. "And you let me stand here trying to convince you when you already know you want to see him. It will turn out well and I will make the cake for your wedding—or maybe it won't be fine and then you will know and he will know and that will be an end to it." Henri shrugged. "But this refusing to even consider a single date is not doing the right thing for either one of you."

"Maybe you're right." Lana couldn't tell Henri how wrong he actually was.

"I am right, you know I am." Henri grinned in delight. "In fact, I am so certain I am right that you and Daniel will make such a beautiful couple that if I am wrong, I will give you coffee free for one whole year!"

"A whole year?" Lana considered and then gave him a crafty smile. "I can drink rather a lot of coffee, you know."

"I know." Henri folded his arms over his chest, confident he'd won. "I am not a gambling man."

"We'll see." Lana picked up the card.

NOT THE red dress. Not suitable for this occasion. Lana threw the hanger onto her bed and searched the wardrobe again. Trousers? Not the right tone. If she wore white, she'd be sure to spill coffee down the front. Not that she'd ever done such a thing before, but her hands were already trembling. The mini? Too short. Too suggestive for a first meeting, even though this was the second.

The decision was too difficult. Lana hurled the skirt in the direction of the bed to join the reject pile.

She reached for a purple dress and stopped short. Damn it all! She'd almost forgotten her meeting with the photographer today. She always wore black for that, allowing her to concentrate on the garments and accessories being shot without becoming distracted by the colors of her own outfit.

This wasn't a date, Lana reminded herself. It was a pre-date date to see if there would ever even be a date. Because she'd never actually had a date before, she wouldn't know, but maybe all women went through this agony of indecision over what to wear. However, the entire point of scheduling their meeting for today was that she had the valid excuse of her job to cut it short if things went bad.

When in doubt, go with black. Her wrap dress was a lightweight crêpe wool and very simple with a V-neck and bracelet-length sleeves.

The dress was flowy enough for her to move around easily for work, but nice enough for a not-date. Lana cinched her waist with a suede belt and then pulled on black flat-heeled boots (easy to run in if it came to that) that came up over her knees. She twisted a scarf around her neck and then raced into the bathroom to put up her hair to get it out of the way.

She never did a smoky eye for the day. Her brows and lashes were black and thick. She needed only a bit of liner and shadow. At the last moment, she decided on a red lip. Might as well add one spot of bright color. Then she worried that was sending the wrong message. Wasn't red the color of passion? Or blood. The word popped into her mind, but she tried to banish it. Not thinking about blood today.

She stared at herself in the mirror. "Remind me why I'm doing this again." Apparently her reflection refused to answer on the grounds it might incriminate itself, because her lips weren't moving.

Lana checked her watch and ran for the door, grabbing a jacket and her bag on the way.

THIS TIME when Daniel looked in at the window of the café, Lana was there, looking stunning and slightly nervous sitting in a booth by the window. She was leafing through a fashion magazine and sipping a coffee.

Henri must have seen Daniel blocking the light. He looked up and smiled when Daniel came in. Daniel paused for a moment, undecided whether to go to the counter for coffee or directly to Lana. He liked coffee but she was better than caffeine. Besides, the coffee wouldn't run away.

Lana looked up, her eyes sparkling when she saw him.

Daniel couldn't suppress a grin of delight. To hell with the coffee. Before he sat down, he offered Lana a single purple orchid. The florist had cut the stem before inserting the blossom into a floral water tube. "Lana. We meet again. This is for you."

"Merci." Lana's fingers were cool against his as she accepted the flower.

"Thank you for agreeing to see me."

"I did so as a favor to Henri."

He'd forgotten the rich timbre of her voice. "I owe him, then." A lot. Daniel sat down, forgetting all about coffee. "It's an orchid, a cymbidium." The florist had called it a corsage, but Lana tucked the flower into her belt at her waist, where it glowed in brilliant contrast against the black of her dress.

"It's lovely, but you're not still thinking of me in Chinese, are you?"

"You remembered." Encouraged by that, Daniel smiled. "I was thinking of you in the language of flowers."

"What a lovely way to be thought about." Lana stroked a petal with one finger.

"I like to imagine two lovers who are forced to meet only under the strict regard of a chaperone who is so near they can never speak freely. Their eyes meet, full of unspoken messages. The only way to communicate what they feel is through the Victorian romantic tradition of symbolism. One would hand the other a flower and their heartfelt sentiments would be clear without a word being said."

"A very romantic tale. And what do orchids mean in this tradition of symbolism?"

Daniel had planned out the specific words he wanted her to hear. "The orchid is a symbol of love, beauty, and refinement. Although they look delicate, they are far tougher than most people think, and they're very adaptable. In ancient Greece they were associated with virility." He flashed her an impish smile. "They also symbolize proud and glorious femininity."

"If you just thought all that up, I'm very impressed." Her mouth curved into a smile, but she didn't laugh.

He shook his head. "Memorized it. I didn't want to stammer and stutter and say something awkward."

"You did very well."

Daniel looked up when Henri put a cup of coffee in front of him. "Merci, Henri," he said meaningfully.

Henri turned slightly so Lana couldn't see his face and gave Daniel a wink.

DANIEL LOOKED better than she remembered. He didn't offer his hand for her to shake. Even when he handed Lana the flower, she was the one who brushed his fingers ever so slightly. Even that brief contact sent a delicious shiver down her spine. She couldn't remember the last time anyone other than the dwarfs had touched her. When Lana stuck the flower into her belt, she took the opportunity to peek under the table. Daniel's feet were tucked way back under his seat. Apparently he wasn't planning on playing footsie. She relaxed slightly, although she kept her feet safely on her side.

"There is something you should know," Lana said.

"I am all ears."

She stared into her coffee cup and then looked up to the glow in his eyes. And chickened out. "I'm not good at relationships."

"Another thing to add to the growing list of what we have in common." Daniel chuckled. "I haven't won any trophies in that arena either."

"Then we should probably call this off, given our track records." Lana grabbed her bag and prepared to flee. All of a sudden, she had cold feet and didn't want to wait around for the consequences.

"Or maybe we shouldn't." His eyes crinkled when he smiled. "What about your friends the dwarfs? You're in a relationship with them."

"The dwarfs and I are just friends. I can do friends."

"So what if we start as just friends and see what happens?"

Daniel didn't try to pressure her. He just waited for her decision.

In the interval, Henri came to the table to refill their cups. Then he turned his back to Daniel to give Lana a wink and a self-satisfied smirk.

Daniel picked up his cup, holding it in both hands. Watching his long slender fingers cradle the porcelain gave Lana the shivers when she thought about those hands on her body. She pushed the thought away. Far away.

And realized she'd completely lost the thread of the conversation until Daniel went on.

"Maybe neither of us trust easily. Bad things happen in life."

"To you too?" Lana was curious as to what answer he would give. Until now, Daniel had appeared to be so confident and at ease that she envied his assurance. But her question seemed to trigger some uncomfortable memory for him. He stared out the window with his jaw clenched as if seeing something that disturbed him.

Until then Lana had gone back and forth about him. The façade of his strength revealed none of his secrets, but now she remembered his reaction to the dropped plate, and that made him more accessible somehow.

"Bad things happen to everyone at some time, I suppose. You can either become a hermit or take a chance again."

"That cave is sounding pretty good."

"Been there." An undertone of bitterness colored his voice. "It was a long hibernation for me, but winter's over now." He looked directly at her. "Maybe for you too."

Lana touched the orchid again. "So you're saying perhaps it's spring."

"Maybe. If that's what we choose." His smile was warmer than that of just a friend.

"As long as it's understood that nothing will come of one single date."

"Just two friends having dinner, getting to know a little about each other," he promised.

"We might want different things."

"We don't have to be sure right now of what we might want in the future. We can take it as it comes. Let's wait and see how one single dinner turns out. Maybe we'll hate each other." Daniel paused for a moment. "But I don't think we will."

"I went to your website. You're a very good painter."

"Thank you." He dipped his head in a quick bow.

"But I don't really know anything about you. Why should I even bother with you?"

He leaned back and stretched both arms over the back of the bench seat. "Ask me anything. I'm game."

"What do you like to eat?"

"Just about anything but snails and worms. Other than that, I'm very open-minded."

Lana laughed, remembering the song he'd mentioned about eating worms. "What's your favorite color?"

"Right out of the gate with the heavy guns. I change my mind every day. Too many delicious colors to choose from and a few I don't care for all that much. But today it's red." Daniel stared at her mouth.

Nervously, Lana licked her lips. "What makes you angry?" *And what do you do when you get angry? Do you lash out with your fists?* But she didn't say that bit aloud.

His eyes opened wide in surprise and a line formed between his brows as he gave it some thought. "Injustice, I guess. That might be hard to believe considering what I—" Daniel broke off abruptly and then hurried to close the gap. "For instance when people judge others by the color of their skin or whatever other meaningless difference some idiot takes offense to. We all want pretty much the same things. Once our basic survival needs are met, we want some sort of connection with another human being. To feel wanted. That we're not alone. To be known."

Lana shivered. That was more true than he could possibly know. "What scares you? What makes you feel weak or vulnerable?"

"Oof, that's hitting below the belt." Daniel shifted in his seat and brought his arms in tight across his chest. "I hate to say it, but my own insecurities sometimes cause me to do things that I... regret later."

"Regret how?"

"Oh, just making a fool of myself."

65

"You appear perfectly confident to me."

"You should see behind the mask. You might be surprised."

Although his tone was light, Lana got the impression that she'd touched a sore spot. Good to know she wasn't alone in that.

"Why did you ask me to come here today?"

"To beg you to reconsider banishing me from your kingdom. Or at least tell me why. Won't you give me a chance to prove I'm not like other people?"

"What other people?"

"The ones who hurt you. Male or female."

"I didn't say anyone had."

"You said you weren't good at relationships."

"But that could be all on me."

"It could, but I highly doubt it. And just in case you hadn't noticed, I'd like to point out that I'm being a gentleman and not asking you the same questions because you haven't invited me to."

A trill of alarm rang in Lana's mind. "I didn't, did I?"

"I can take a hint. You want to go slow, and that's fine with me. No secrets spilled until the time is right." Daniel picked up his coffee and took a sip.

Lana had to wonder what he saw when he looked at her. She glanced at her watch. "Speaking of time."

"Wait, you haven't given me an answer yet. Do we have a date?"

She smiled. "Very well, I'll meet you. Such persistence deserves a reward."

"Tonight?"

"I'm busy tonight. Friday. At eight."

"If I had a previous engagement, I would cancel it, but I don't. I've cleared my calendar for you. May I pick you up?"

"We'll meet." She named a popular restaurant located in a busy district. Now it was up to him to see they got a table. Let him work for it if he wanted a date that much.

He was beaming at her. "I will rendezvous with you there."

"And now I must run. I'm late for work." Lana stood up to go. "Thank you for breakfast."

He got to his feet hurriedly when she did. "It was entirely my pleasure."

She held in her grin until she was out the door.

A date! She had a date!

Lana smiled all the way to work, and especially whenever she looked down at the orchid at her waist.

"WHAT ARE you playing at? Paper dolls?" Catharine stared at the table where Lana had arranged pieces of white foam core to make a miniature three-sided room. An artist's armature stood in the middle with one hand on its hip in a fashion pose.

"That would be fun, but I'm plotting out my shoot so when Pavlo gets here, I'm prepared."

Catharine gave a quick nod of approval. "Haute Macabre on a budget, right? What happened to the forests?"

"As I went through the rack, I realized all of the dresses have quite a bit of detail and ornamentation. A forest would add too much distracting texture to the background. This is a new concept."

"And the horns?" Catharine raised her brows.

"Oh, we're keeping the horns. And the teased hair." Lana pushed a folded piece of paper into her miniature set.

"What's that supposed to be?" Catharine waited, puzzled.

Lana turned on a flashlight and set it on the table in front of the paper. The light threw a shadow onto the back wall, turning the jagged paper into an uncanny silhouette of a rocky horizon. "Pretend those are rocks jutting out into the sea. I think we'll bring sand into the studio for the models to stand in. Or maybe we can do a sheet of plexi on top with water underneath so the models look as if they're levitating. We'll add a few twisted branches and pebbles, but severely curated. Organic objects to contrast with the intentional craft of the dressmaking. I'll have the girls backlit so we can spotlight the important details and blur the edges of the garments into the background." The painting on Daniel's card popped into her head, and Lana hid a smile as she realized what had inspired that bit of direction.

"Won't their heels sink into the sand?" Catharine asked.

"Always the pragmatist, Catharine, but you make a good point." Lana chuckled. "We'll have the models go barefoot and they can either hold the shoes or we'll place them someplace meaningful on the set."

"Sounds a bit surrealistic, but I like how you describe it." Catharine shifted and looked at the shadow from a different angle. "It just looks like a bit of crumpled paper until you put that light on it."

"Isabelle said on a budget, and paper is cheap. We'll probably use some colored gels on the back wall, something from the opposite side of the color wheel to make each garment stand out. Maybe one side dark and the other light." Lana picked up a piece of paper and held it up to cast a shadow on the left side of her mini set. "This will be cool. I can't wait to tell—" She stopped speaking and pressed her lips together.

"That telltale smirk says somebody is in a good mood," Catharine observed. "Don't tell me you're finally going on a date at last?"

"Why would you ever think that?"

"Doll, when a girl is looking forward to a special date, she gets a certain kind of glow. I've never noticed that sort of glow on you, and it's nice to see it for once. You're such a beautiful girl, but you don't get out enough. Live a little! Let go and have some fun."

In the face of Catharine's enthusiastic support, Lana tried to let go of her doubts. After all, she and Daniel had agreed this was a onetime thing. Not a big thing, merely a chance to get to know each other better. No clothing would flutter to the floor, and her secret would still be hers. And perhaps Daniel would prove to be as open-minded as he claimed. She would never know if she didn't test the water.

Lana smiled in satisfaction as she studied her folded-up bit of paper casting a giant shadow. "I will do my best."

"And that's all anyone can ask." With a delighted grin, Catharine went to the door, gave Lana an enthusiastic thumbs-up, and departed.

Now all Lana had to do was tell the dwarfs. Her smile faded and she plumped down in her chair. That was one conversation she was not looking forward to.

CHAPTER 6

DOM PACED in Lana's living room, waiting to try to talk her out of this madness. Terry was more at ease, lounging on the sofa watching the television with the sound turned off. Colin was there in spirit only, because he had a dinner booked for that evening, but he had told Dom not to do anything he wouldn't. Dom took that to mean he could not actually chain Lana down and forbid her to go. Colin was always more temperate in his approach.

Lana pulled back the curtain that guarded her bedroom and came out to show herself off. She wore a dress of floaty chiffon. The neckline was daringly slit to the waist, but her chest was mostly concealed by wispy layers of silk draping in soft pleats gathered in at the waistband. A chunky necklace with faceted glass gems of greens and blues hugged her throat, and her hair was twisted into an updo, loose curls framing her face. The skirt swirled gracefully around her legs like sea-foam when she gave the dwarfs a spin. "Do you approve?"

"Of how you look, yes. Of what you're doing, no way." Dom cracked his knuckles loudly enough to make sure everyone within a two-block radius heard the crunch.

"I like the contrast of the hardness of the necklace against the softness of the fabric." Terry used the remote to turn off the TV.

"Dopey, did you just offer an unprompted editorial fashion comment?" Lana raised her hand to touch the necklace. "Don't tell me Martine has you hooked on fashion."

Ignoring her question, Terry stabbed an accusatory finger at the neckline. "How*ever*, you're showing far too much skin for a first date."

"Prude."

"It's the latest trend, Terry, but we're not here to discuss the pros and cons of her outfit." Dom frowned at Terry and then he turned on Lana. "This date is another story. Have you gone off your trolley? Showing that much skin on a first date?" Dom threw his hands in the air in disgust. "Back up, wait, wait, wait. Don't even bother to answer that. I don't care about your dress. What the hell are you thinking even *having* a first date to begin with?"

"Barmy." Terry circled his finger at his temple. "She's living in a fairy tale."

"I'm simply going out for dinner." Twisting around, Lana angled to see her reflection in the mirror over the fireplace. She adjusted the necklace so it lay flat. "We've both agreed that nothing is going to happen."

Dom blocked the door as if she was going to make a break for it. "Men always want something to happen. If you think nothing will, you're out of touch with reality."

"That *is* sort of the definition of a fairy tale." Terry spoke in an undertone.

"You don't know anything about him." Dom's voice rose.

"Neither do you," Lana pointed out. "But by all means, come along. I already told Daniel to expect it. As long as I can come along on your next date with Gilles."

"Whatever for?" Dom stared.

"You cockblock me, I cockblock you. It's only fair."

Terry looked at Dom. "If we're there, she can't do the nasty."

"That's the definition of cockblock. And I can't do it even if I wanted to. I didn't shave my legs."

"Oh, so that's why you offered. And here I thought you were being nice to Dom." Terry bent and raked his hand up her leg. "Good thing she's wearing stockings. She ain't lying about the gams. Stubble city."

"What the fuck are you talking about?" Dom rolled his eyes in exasperation.

"Right, you're a poofter, you wouldn't know this. Tell him, Lana."

"Birth control device for a first date. If you don't shave your legs, you won't take off your clothes."

"Knowing you didn't shave makes me feel a little better." Terry blew out a soundless whistle from between pursed lips. "What makes me feel worse is that you even thought of it. That means you're thinking of it, and once the thinking about it starts, safety flies out the window."

"What is with you guys? First Colin tries to sign me up on a dating site and you, Terry, tell me not to give up hope, and now you're having a cow over one date?"

"I'm having second thoughts. It's easier to cheer you on when the date is hypothetical, but this is the real thing," Terry said. "I'm starting to hyperventilate a little."

"Deep breaths, Ter." Lana patted him on the back.

"Did you tell this guy yet?" Dom narrowed his eyes at Lana, although he found it hard to keep up the menace factor. She looked so pretty.

"His name is Daniel."

"And did you tell him?"

Lana turned away from Dom to look at herself in the mirror again. "Maybe I shouldn't go after all."

"So that's a no." Dom knew her well enough to know that. She never could figure out a way to do it. Not that there was an easy way.

Lana picked up her evening bag and played with the clasp. "I could tell him when I show up."

"Right, that'll fly. Hi, fella, thanks for the invitation to dinner. By the way, I'm a guy pretending to be a girl. Shall we dine?" Dom threw up his hands in disgust. "What could possibly go wrong after that?"

Lana giggled at that scenario. "Maybe I'll try to clue him in a bit more subtly."

Terry suddenly relented. "You never go anywhere but Colin's. You haven't even been out to dinner with us in a proper restaurant in over three years."

Exasperated, Dom glared back and forth at both of them. "Back to the business at hand, please. Lana, you're an adult. Much as I'd like to lock you in your room and throw away the key until you're seventy, I can't forbid you to meet this guy. But I'm asking you as a friend who worries about you, after everything we've said, are you still going to meet him?"

"Yes." Finally Lana stopped playing with her bag and looked up, her mouth set in a mulish line. "I know I'm taking a chance, Dom. I know this whole thing is my fault for being different. I'm under no delusion that Daniel is going to ride in on a white horse and sweep me off to a castle and we'll live happily ever after. I could be wrong, but I don't think he's going to harm me if he finds out. I don't plan on telling him tonight either. I just want to go out on one date. One date! Is that too much to ask? He doesn't know my last name. I didn't give him my phone number. I just want one night with a man who looks at me as if I'm the most beautiful, desirable woman in the world. And after Cinderella gets back from the ball, she'll put on her designer rags and go back to her fashion drudgery without complaint. Sorry, Happy, I'm going."

"It's *not* your fault. You're fine as you are, it's other people who are crazy." Dom wished she could have everything she wanted, but he was still afraid. He gave her a reluctant smile. "I get it and I hope the date turns out as you wish, but if you're going, we're going too. We'll be right behind you, so don't do anything you don't want us to see you doing."

"Yes, Mum." Lana's cheeks turned pink. "Still going."

"This is no laughing matter, Snow White." Giddy. She was just plain giddy and not thinking straight, but that's why Dom tried to talk her out of it. His little arguments hadn't worked, and now it was his job to keep her safe. "We're not trying to spoil your fun. You know we're on your side."

"Always have been," Terry said. "Even if it doesn't always sound like it."

"Daniel may already know too much." Dom's frown creased his forehead. "We may have to kill him."

"That's a bit extreme, isn't it?" Terry stuck a finger into his collar and swallowed audibly.

"Grow a set," Dom snapped. "I wasn't speaking literally. We'll do whatever it takes to—"

"You murder him before I meet him and you will curse this day for the rest of your lives, got it, dwarfs?" Lana pointed at each of them in turn and gave them a stony glare.

"Let's hope that's the only reason we curse this day." Dom caught the hint of steel in her voice. Even worse, Lana glowed with anticipation, and he hadn't seen her like that for a long time. He didn't want to be the one to snuff it out. "If you're going to show off that dress, we should go, then. I have a taxi waiting downstairs."

Lana laughed. "So you knew I was going anyway?"

"I know you better than you think, Lana. You be careful or I will never forgive you."

"I'll be careful. I promise." Her smile faded. "Dom, I know what you're trying to say. Yes, he followed me, but he apologized for it. He didn't do it again. When I talked to him, I looked into his eyes."

"So he's got nice eyes," Terry muttered.

"He does, but if you don't trust him, you can trust me," Lana said. "I can take care of myself now."

"I hope so, Lana." Dom was only slightly comforted by the hug Lana gave him.

KNOWING TWO of the dwarfs were dogging her footsteps as she reached the rendezvous did help Lana's confidence. Daniel was waiting outside, leaning against the brick building. What he wasn't doing was checking his watch and looking around nervously. In fact, he looked self-assured, altogether too much so to suit Lana. She decided to let Daniel wait a bit longer to pay him for that.

Daniel's casual pose did nothing to showcase his obvious athleticism. He looked quick, like he ran or played sports, but the times she had been close to him, Daniel had moved his hands with deliberate care, and he stayed outside the invisible circle she'd drawn around herself. That sensitivity increased her level of comfort with him.

Every time Lana saw him, she liked him more. Even with Daniel's face in repose, he always looked as if he were smiling or about to. If only they were already lovers so she could leap into Daniel's arms and beg to be taken back to his place as he'd suggested. Even though the thought of putting on such a show for the dwarfs made her snicker, Lana would not be going to Daniel's place any time soon. Especially now, as the dwarfs would probably dart out of the shadows, latch onto her, and refuse to let go. The idea of them all roiling about in a slapstick tussle made Lana giggle again.

Perhaps Dom was right after all. This meeting with Daniel was contrary to the rules she lived her life by. A shiver of fear chilled her, and she pulled her jacket tighter. She could still change her mind, go home, and hope Daniel got the message. The dwarfs would celebrate. She could probably even get them to pay the cab fare. After all, Daniel had said that if the answer was no, he would go away and eat worms.

What madness had driven her to come? Lana looked down at her dress and sighed. Was it really as simple as Dom had suggested? A desire to show off this outfit? Of course not. Whatever drew Lana to this man was potent enough to override a lifetime of caution. Might as well go through with it now that she was here. Maybe the euphoria bubbling up inside would die down after more contact with Daniel. If absence made the heart grow fonder, what was the opposite? Familiarity breeds contempt?

The smell of grilled steak reminded her how hungry she was. Finally, Lana took a deep breath and prepared to meet her fate. She stepped out of the shadows and went to meet Daniel, painfully aware of the dwarfs watching her every move.

THE LATER she was, the more importance this meeting took on. The last time Daniel had asked a person out with no motive other than attraction had been very long ago. Chances were that Lana wouldn't show up. That she had agreed at all surprised him after her statement that she didn't date. He dared to hope that perhaps she was more attracted than she seemed.

A glimpse of one of the dwarfs trying to conceal himself in the shadows while ignoring the light shining on his feet alerted Daniel to Lana's presence before he saw her. First came the click of her heels on the pavement, and then he breathed in a whiff of her scent before turning to face her.

"Bonsoir." Lana smiled at him.

"Bonsoir." In her heels, she was as tall as he, so they stood eye to eye. "I hope you're hungry."

The comment hung in the air between them, full of unasked potential.

"I often am at this time of the evening."

"I like your outfit," Daniel said.

"I do too." She smoothed the fabric of her skirt with one hand. "Merci."

"I reserved a table. They're holding it for us."

"Really? They never do that." She allowed him to guide her into the restaurant.

"I was very polite when I asked."

She laughed. "I'm certain you were. It probably had nothing to do with a certain number of euros changing hands."

Daniel grinned. "Not at all. Should I have gotten a table for your friends?"

"We'll let them manage on their own."

When Daniel caught the concierge's eye, he smiled and came to lead them to their table.

Daniel held Lana's chair for her and helped her remove her jacket. Then he rounded the table and sat facing her. "Shall I order wine?"

"Are you hoping to get me drunk?" Lana picked up the menu and peeked at him over the top.

"I shan't need to. When you say yes, I want you sentient, alert, and completely willing."

"So far I'm in no danger of succumbing."

"I'll win you over."

"That sounds cocky."

The waiter came over with a wine menu and asked what they wanted to order.

Daniel consulted the menu. He looked at Lana, eyebrows raised. "Do you have a preference for red or white?"

"Red would be fine."

Daniel made his selection and handed the menu back to the waiter.

"Not cocky. Confident." He smiled at her. "What have you got to lose? At the very least I will treat you to a nice meal, even if the conversation flags."

The smile left her eyes and her chin went up defiantly. "And then you plan to collect in return for the price of the dinner?"

"You're in the driver's seat. If you tell me to go away, you'll never see me again," he reminded her gently. "Besides, you're worth more than that."

The dimples in her cheeks quivered into existence. "Yes, I am." She touched the choker at her throat.

"That is a magnificently decadent necklace. Is it real?"

"Real costume jewelry. Alas, the crown jewels are in the wash."

Her fingers trembled a bit. Daniel pretended not to notice. The waiter returned and poured the wine for Daniel's approval. He took a sip and nodded.

After the waiter ecstatically described the choices for that evening and had taken their orders, Daniel waited a moment before saying, "You should be decked out in emeralds and rubies and gold, with your coloring."

"Not on my budget."

"You never told me what you do for work."

"You never asked." Lana took a sip of her wine and smirked at him.

"I'm asking now," Daniel said when it became clear she wasn't going to offer the information unprompted.

"I work for a fashion magazine."

"Editor in chief? Stylist? Photographer?"

A note of derision sounded in her laugh. "The very subbest of subeditors."

"Do you like it?"

A fire of enthusiasm lit her eyes. "Fashion is my life. I can't imagine doing anything else."

"I could tell. You have a certain je ne sais quoi that is beyond beauty," Daniel said.

Her eyes widened in surprise. "What a lovely compliment."

"It's only the truth. And what does a subeditor do?"

"I bring the coffee and occasionally contribute a paragraph of musings upon the fashionable vagaries of socks."

"Socks can be very important." Daniel tried not to laugh. In his wildest dreams, and he'd had some about her, he'd never pictured them discussing socks on their first date.

"When you consider socks are almost invariably covered by shoes, their impact is greatly diminished. Even more so under boots. But it was charming of you to say so."

"Not at all, when you consider socks are the gateway to shoes. And besides, we all take our shoes off at some point, displaying our socks to the world. When we get home, we kick off our shoes and sigh in relief. Shoes can be uncomfortable, but socks generally are not."

"Unless your toe is poking through a hole." Lana's eyes twinkled with amusement. "Socks can be a decorative statement and come in a vast variety of colors and patterns. They can be chic or amusing or practical or all at once. Or completely impractical, for instance, toe socks. Colored socks with suits are very in for men right now."

"Already you have persuaded me to question my own sartorial choices in socks, so you may consider yourself influential in your field. Until now, I have tended to stick with dull neutrals. What should I wear to impress you?"

"That is supposing we should ever reach terms where I am in a position to evaluate your socks," Lana said.

"When," he corrected her and then stretched out his foot. "See? Plain black."

"Oh, but neutrals don't have to be boring. Recently I saw a men's sock in tones of gray with a subtle contrasting line of navy running vertically up the outside of the leg, displaying three discreet turquoise circles judiciously spaced at pleasing intervals along the line."

"Your attention to detail fascinates me. Clearly you've made a study of the subject. Do you knit the dwarfs socks for Christmas?"

Lana threw her head back and laughed. "No, I usually find a nonfiction book for Happy, because he's a journalist, and a bottle of wine for Dopey. For Bashful, whatever the latest food trend dictates: a chateaubriand or perhaps a white truffle from Italy. He is a chef."

Score one on the reporter who followed him, although not for the reason he'd thought. Daniel gave himself a mental fist pump. "I would have thought the wine would go to Bashful."

"I wouldn't dare choose wine for him and earn his unending contempt if I guessed wrong."

"And what does Dopey do for work?"

"He's a real estate agent. He works mainly with expats."

"Wish I'd known him when I moved here."

"You don't know him now."

"True." Daniel straightened his tie. "Do you dress yourself?"

"What?" Lana stared at him in surprise.

"Your appearance is so incredibly soignée, I find it difficult to believe you've been relegated to meditations on the lowly sock. I mean, you certainly are knocking mine off." He gave her an appreciative glance. "But your attention to the color and fit of your clothing and accessories is superb. And you've mastered proportion, one of the most difficult elements of dress that seems to elude many women."

Lana raised her brows in surprise. "It's not often I meet someone who understands and values proportion."

"Does that mean I get a reward for noticing?"

"What have you in mind?"

"Tell me what you really do." A flutter of nerves beat a tattoo in his palms. Maybe she would reveal one of her secrets at last. He found it hard to believe anyone as intelligent could remain a subeditor for long.

She laughed in capitulation. "Clever of you. Actually I'm a stylist. I analyze garments and accessories such as shoes, jewelry, and bags. Then I come up with a concept and direct the photo shoots for the magazine. I work with the hair and makeup people, choose the models, and make sure the garments are fitted to them. But I did get my start as a subeditor, and my first assignment really was about socks."

"I bow to your credentials. Could I ask you to direct me to a purveyor of socks interesting enough to meet with your approval?"

"That I could do."

The waiter arrived with their food.

THE QUIET street was both a relief and a danger to Lana when they emerged. The restaurant had been too crowded for any but the most surface conversation. She had enjoyed their verbal jousting, but now what?

She rubbed one stubbly leg against the other to reinforce that there would be no going back to either place, no matter how comfortable she might feel with this man. Horrified that the thought even occurred to her, Lana remained silent. She should probably say good night and go straight home.

"Could I entice you to join me in a walk by the river?" Daniel asked.

"What a perfect suggestion." Shocked at her own words, Lana bit her lip. What was she thinking? Nothing was more romantic—or more perilous—than walking by the Seine at night in spring. The air was a bit cooler tonight than was comfortable, and she should have used that as an excuse to refuse. Instead Lana buttoned her jacket. "I should like to, although I would rather not hike all the way there in these." She turned her foot to show off the heel. If she had to run later, better save her feet now.

"We'll grab a taxi. There's a stand around the corner." Daniel led the way and opened the door to the first car in the lineup.

After they got in, Daniel spoke to the driver. "Un moment, s'il vous plaît." Then he twisted to look out the rear window.

"Why are we just sitting here?"

Daniel pointed through the window. "Waiting for the dwarfs to engage a cab for themselves. I thought of reserving one for them, but then I thought they might suspect me of directing the driver to take them somewhere else."

"It is only polite to wait for them." Lana turned around and tried not to smirk when she saw her friends bundling into the next taxi. "You don't mind them tailing us?"

"Not at all. If it amuses them, it doesn't bother me. My intentions are strictly honorable." Daniel reached for Lana's hand but then checked himself.

Pretending she hadn't noticed, Lana took a mirror out of her bag and touched up her lipstick. Her heart was pounding.

"Ah, we are all ready now." Daniel leaned forward to address the driver. "Allons-y, s'il vous plaît. Pont de l'Archevêché."

Lana held up her mirror to catch sight of the cab tailing them. "Only two of them are on duty. Colin works nights."

"My loss is his customers' gain, I'm sure."

"He is a very fine chef." Lana put away the mirror and lipstick. "His dinner parties are very exclusive, and reservations are out three months."

"Perhaps we should go sometime," Daniel said.

That idea gave Lana a fit of the giggles. She pictured Dom and Terry attending and glowering over the table at her and Daniel....

The taxi ride was a short one. When they arrived, Daniel paid the driver and asked him to wait.

Obviously a quick learner, Daniel offered his hand instead of simply reaching for Lana's. Thankful for the barrier of her gloves, Lana took Daniel's hand. The minute she did so, she realized her mistake.

The heat of Daniel's hand burned through the thin leather and set her on fire. Suddenly Lana was grateful for the camouflage of her skirt, something she usually didn't have to worry about. She tried to focus on the glint of moonlight on the water. And how a cold shower would feel right now.

Daniel swung their clasped hands slightly as they walked, while keeping to a pace suitable for a person in very high heels.

"I love Notre-Dame at night." Lana hoped Daniel hadn't noticed how fast she was breathing. "The way the lights reflect off the surface of the water and the boats float by slowly on the river."

"I love Paris in the springtime," Daniel started to sing softly. He had a good voice.

"*An American in Paris*," Lana teased.

"Awkward lot, aren't we?" Daniel gave her a smile of agreement.

"So far you have put the lie to the myth of the ugly American."

She was relieved when Daniel started to hum again so they didn't have to talk. Lana suddenly remembered the dwarfs were watching them. Devoutly hoping that they wouldn't feel impelled to rescue her at the sight of their clasped hands and start a brawl, Lana kept walking, even though street brawls could be fun and she knew how to run in heels if the gendarmes showed up.

When they reached the center of the bridge, Daniel paused to lean against the stone railing. He turned to face Lana. "I would like to paint you."

Lana took a step back. "As in, take off my clothes to model for you?

"Your face. Your beautiful face."

The way Daniel studied her with no judgment in his eyes was new for Lana.

"I'm staring because I love to watch the way your face changes. You turn your head a little and you look very different."

His considered answer calmed Lana. "Sorry. I thought it was just a cheap come-on."

"Haven't you realized yet I'm not like other men?"

"So far you have behaved yourself rather well," Lana admitted. "Next you're going to say you don't want to fuck me, and that we shall just be friends."

Daniel grinned at her choice of words. "Oh, I do want to fuck you. I most definitely do. But not for bragging rights after storming the citadel. This isn't about conquest. I want you to be sure when you say yes."

"You seem certain it's going to be yes." A bit miffed by Daniel's presumption, Lana almost turned to go, but curiosity got the better of her. "How were you planning to seduce me?"

"I would listen to your voice when you tell me stories about how you grew up. Maybe go to a museum or on a picnic. Or maybe we could picnic *in* the museum and get kicked out for irreverence. Sing love songs to you. Visit old bookstores and search for books on art and fashion. I would eat garlic whenever you did so we could kiss anyway. I would fall on my ass to make you laugh. And then I'd take you to Henri's to remind you that we went out for coffee when we first met."

"Are you always this silly?"

"Before I met you, I pretended to be a surly, misunderstood bad boy. Worked like a charm." Ditching his perfect posture, Daniel slouched and put his hands in his pockets. He gave her a sullen scowl.

When Lana laughed, he laughed with her. "What a droll man you are." Dangerous how much she liked him. "What would you sing?"

"A song that only you can hear because only you make me want to sing it." Daniel started to hum and held out both hands in invitation.

Against her usual instinct of immediate flight, Lana stepped into the circle of Daniel's arms and swayed with him, wishing she could see the romantic picture of them dancing by the river. The scent of early lilies and grass wafted over them as they danced in the moonlight.

Daniel held her loosely. Lana knew she could escape if she wanted to—but she didn't want to.

When Daniel leaned closer, Lana stiffened for a moment and felt him hesitate. Curious as to what he would do, she forced her muscles to relax. Daniel closed his eyes and leaned in closer. Even though Daniel's breath was warm on her face and something hard and wonderful was impressing its shape against Lana's thigh, she backed away.

Daniel opened his eyes. His chest rose and fell quickly, but his arms were relaxed and he made no attempt to constrain Lana. "Would it be okay for me to kiss you now?"

The brief moment of elation dissipated. Lana realized she couldn't wait any longer to make her revelation.

"Wait, Daniel, I need to tell you something first." Her heart racing, Lana was about to blurt out the truth when another taxi pulled up to the curb behind theirs and the horn sounded sharply.

Lana twisted in Daniel's arms to look. "The dwarfs."

"Seems like your coach has arrived." Daniel released Lana and stepped back. His face was flushed with arousal, but he was smiling.

"I'd better go before it turns back into a pumpkin and the mice get restless. I hate to run in glass slippers. They tend to shatter."

"I wouldn't want you to get splinters. I hope that's regret I hear in your voice."

Conscious of the dwarfs' beady stares, Lana took a step toward the taxi. Was that frustration in Daniel's eyes or something else? "It wasn't so bad for a first date."

"Does that mean there will be another?"

"Are you asking?"

"It's an open invitation." Daniel shifted his gaze when the door of the taxi swung open.

Dom hopped out with a scowl on his face, but it wasn't directed at her. Instead he started aggressively toward Daniel, taking up a stance between him and Lana. "Time to go, Lana."

Hands raised in a placating gesture, Daniel backed up another step. He appeared more amused than angry. "I won't stand in your way."

Speaking quietly so Daniel couldn't hear her, Lana muttered, "Dom, you're a dick." She turned back to Daniel. "I need to go with my friends now. Thank you for a wonderful time tonight."

"Will you call me?"

Her irritation with the dwarfs melted at Daniel's obvious eagerness, and she smiled. "Perhaps."

Dom backed up, bumping into Lana and herding her toward the taxi where Terry waited outside, never taking his gaze off Daniel.

"Au revoir." Daniel took a step forward.

"Adieu." Lana felt a tug on her jacket and turned to give Terry the finger. He made a face at her and gestured for her to get in.

Lana seated herself in the taxi and swung her legs in. Before she could say another word, Dom and Terry piled in next to her, squeezing her into the far corner and slammed the door shut.

Terry leaned forward to speak to the driver. "Allez."

As they drove off, Lana twisted around to look at Daniel through the back window. He stood there watching for as long as she could see him.

"WHAT THE hell were you thinking?" Dom forced the words out past his clenched teeth in English, hoping the driver didn't know enough to follow.

"What the hell were *you* thinking?" Lana's answer was a snarl of resentment.

"We told you not to kiss him!" Terry was outraged.

"Well, you were there. He may have attempted to score, but our lips did not touch, remember?"

"But the rest of you was. He had his arms around you!"

She spoke through clenched teeth. "I did not get in this cab because of anything you did or might do. Don't flatter yourselves that you came storming to the rescue. I panicked, all right? I was just about to tell him when you guys rolled up at the wrong time and screwed everything up."

Dom was skeptical. "What were you going to say?"

"I hadn't figured it out yet. You distracted me."

"Maybe you could do it by text." Terry's voice was nervous. "Then you wouldn't be right there where he could reach you when he found out."

"Brilliant, Terry. Then it's in print and he can tell the world." Dom's anxiety died at the anguish on Lana's face. "I'm not sure there is a great way to deliver this kind of news, but at least if you just say it, the words are only air and gone in a breath."

"I never thought it would come to this." Tears welled up in Lana's eyes, and she brushed them away. "I thought I could have fun for just one fucking night, just one!"

Leaning forward across Terry, Dom touched her arm, but she pulled away. "I guess we overstepped a little, but we worry about you. We love you, Lana. We don't want you to be unhappy."

"It's kind of hard to tell from this angle, boys." Lana stared out the window. "I was happy. For a little while."

"But we also don't want you to be dead." When she wouldn't look his way, Dom retreated into his corner. Maybe he could write out something for her to say, but there really was no good way to reveal this secret. She was upset and pissed. At them. Mostly him, if he was honest. And Terry was glaring at him too.

LANA REFUSED to kiss the dwarfs good-bye when they dropped her off. She was furious, both for the interruption and for the warnings that reinforced that she was a freak that no one could ever want. For once they were tactful and didn't insist on accompanying her upstairs.

Safely inside her flat, Lana hurled her bag across the room and choked out an angry sob. She *was* a freak, by "normal" standards, and nobody could want her, but the dwarfs were supposed to be on her side.

And what about her instincts! They should have been telling her to run from Daniel as fast as she could, but they seemed to be malfunctioning. She couldn't believe Daniel meant to harm her, but the consequences for guessing wrong were dire.

Daniel didn't know the truth, and who knew how he would react when he found out. That was why the dwarfs had tailed them tonight.

Without forcing his way and in the most charming manner possible, Daniel had already managed to invade Lana's perfect, lonely little world. After a lifetime building thick walls to hide behind, somehow Daniel seemed to have already stormed the castle. The thought terrified Lana—and thrilled her. How had she allowed this to happen?

The feel of Daniel's arms around her, the intent look in his eyes when he leaned in for a kiss—a kiss that Lana wanted desperately…. She wrapped her arms around herself and held on tightly. Her throat was tight as she fought her tears. More than attention, Lana needed someone to want her.

Looking down, Lana took a swat at the cock tenting the skirt of her dress. Frustrated by her body's betrayal, she tore off her clothing and fled into the bathroom. She turned on the cold water in the shower and leaned against the wall, goose bumps popping out on her skin. She cried in silence over a man she really didn't know and couldn't have.

CHAPTER 7

IF LANA didn't answer her own phone, Catharine would assume she was busy, pick up at the ninth ring, and take a message. Lana counted the rings until they stopped.

A quick knock sounded. Catharine opened the door and stuck her head in, her face a bit stern. "Your friend Dom is on the phone."

"Thank you." Lana waited until Catharine closed the door and then picked up. "What?" She spoke in English. Safer. Although many people at the magazine did as well, most of them weren't that fluent.

"Yeah, good morning to you too," Dom grumbled. "Has he called?"

"Yes."

"Did you talk to him?"

"What's the point? Eventually he'll get the message."

"He hasn't so far."

"It's only been a week."

"Lana...." The line hummed while Dom went silent for a minute. "I'm sorry this is so fucked-up."

"Until this happened, I was doing fine. Working, living my life. Going shopping. Seeing you lot whenever."

"You sound miserable. And exhausted."

Lana closed her eyes and leaned her head on her hand. "It is exhausting, having to hide the most important part of myself. Usually I don't think too much about it, but now I have to be on guard all the time and I'm watching every little thing I do at work. I have no close friends except the three of you dwarfs, and even when I hate you, I have to talk to you because there is no one else who knows!"

"Believe me, Lana, I know. Being gay isn't something I broadcast at work either. It's nobody's business."

"Like me. I'm nobody's business." And at this rate, she never would be. Her throat ached. She didn't want to cry all over Dom, especially when she was angry as fuck with him.

"I know." Dom's voice was gentler. "And now we all have boyfriends and girlfriends and not as much time for you. We're sort of shoving it in your face."

"Yes. You are." She kept it short. Lana couldn't trust her voice not to give out. Pity was not what she wanted from Dom.

"If you really like this guy—although let me just say, I smell something hinky about him—but if you do want to see him again, the only way is to come clean," Dom said.

"I *know* that, but how? Just what am I supposed to do, Dom? Lower my voice and announce I'm really a man? Say 'hey, it's a sausage-fest all up in here under the skirt'?" Every *s* slithered out of her mouth as a hiss, and Lana wished Dom was in front of her so she could bite him. She wanted to bite *something*.

"After all this time, you still haven't figured out how to tell a guy?" Now he sounded impatient. Argumentative.

"After a few disastrous tries, I usually never let it get this far. I nip it in the bud early on and they give up."

"So say no already and tell him to keep walking."

Lana struggled to work out how to explain this. Dom already thought she was in too deep. How could she justify, even to herself, taking a chance on Daniel? The risk came down to intuition, and she could never convince practical Dom to trust something as ephemeral as her feelings. Especially as she could be wrong.

"What's the difference this time, Lana?" Dom's voice changed again. He was quieter, calmer, as if he might actually hear her.

She had to admit the truth to herself and to Dom if he was going to help her. "Because this time I don't want to say no."

Dom's sigh was audible over the phone. "I thought so. Listen, babe, the sooner you tell him, the better."

"It's past time for me to tell him. Usually I don't even get to a first date, and I'd like to point out I was on the verge of telling him when you charged in without looking, so if you hadn't jumped the gun, we wouldn't be having this conversation and Daniel would most likely be history by now."

"I'm glad to hear you were going to tell him, but how the hell was I supposed to know? You looked like you were going to kiss him!"

"Defensive, Dom?"

"Well, yeah."

"Good."

"Bitch."

"Damn right! So are you going to help me out here?"

"Let me see if I can write something for you. I'm assuming you want to let him down easy."

"Tends to be safer for me." Lana dropped her voice to a whisper. "Sticks and stones can break my bones, and so can a straight man whose masculinity is threatened by finding out the girl he wants to fuck is a boy in a dress and sporting an operational dick."

"Okay, I think I got the gist. 'Sorry, I'm a guy, hope I didn't break your penis, good day and don't bother ringing again.' I'll get back to you."

"Thanks."

"You don't sound too enthusiastic."

"Fuck off, Dom." Lana pressed the button to end the call. First-world problems with modern technology. One couldn't slam the phone in someone's ear to communicate just how thoroughly pissed off one was with them. Unsatisfying.

She stared at the collection of bracelets on her desk. Lana hated them all. The phone on her desk rang again and she started a hand toward it automatically. Then she pulled back and covered her ears. Eventually it stopped after nine rings.

Her door opened and Catharine marched to her desk clutching a handful of messages. "Lana, is there some reason you're not answering your phone?"

"I'm busy." Even Lana could tell her tone was sullen. She didn't look at Catharine.

"Just tell me who you're trying to avoid and I'll get rid of them for you. Isabelle—you remember her, dragon lady, the creative director, your *boss*—wants to know if you're taking the day off because you missed two of her calls and didn't ring her back. The photographer called. The makeup stylist rang. One of the designers called. Your friends Terry and Colin phoned, and your boyfriend called." Catharine slapped the messages onto the desk and used one of the heavier bracelets to anchor them, after checking to be sure her tag with the designer's name was still securely attached.

"I don't have a boyfriend."

"Well, that explains why you're sulking and snapping and not answering the phone. Why don't you phone Daniel and let *him* in on that little secret so he'll stop ringing? It's not nice to leave someone hanging like that."

"I didn't tell you his name."

Visibly irked, Catharine stabbed the messages with a stiff forefinger. "He did. And he left his number. He said to tell you he won't call again. If you want to speak to him, you'll have to call him."

Lana got up and crossed to the window. She wrapped her arms tightly around herself and stared down at the street below, hoping Catharine would get the message and leave her alone.

She jumped when a warm hand landed on her back.

"Take it easy, doll. Tell me why you have your panties in a bunch."

"I wear a thong."

Catharine snickered. "Should have figured that. No VPL. Look, I know our friendship doesn't extend outside this office, and that's okay. I get that you like your privacy, but I make a good wailing wall because I listen, offer good advice only if asked, and nothing you say will go further than me. I won't even tell my husband."

Lana didn't answer. Even though Catharine probably wouldn't have a problem with it, this was a tough bridge to cross. Her boss Isabelle, on the other hand….

"If you don't want to tell me, that's all right too, but you need to pull yourself together. The way you're acting is just not professional. If you can't put your personal problems aside, then perhaps you shouldn't be here. Take a few days off and try to work it out."

The note of rebuke in Catharine's voice resonated with Lana. "I apologize, Catharine. You're perfectly right, and I shouldn't make you run interference for me without even asking you to do it."

"A little warning would have been nice. Let me know if you want me to tell Daniel to stop if he calls again. Because I'll do it if you can't."

Lana trembled as Catharine rubbed a comforting little circle on her back. Down near her waist, because Catharine was more than a head shorter than Lana, but she still appreciated the gesture and human contact.

"When I was a little b—" Horrified, Lana stopped short and clapped both hands over her mouth. The word *boy* almost came out. She must be really off her game.

"When you were a little baby? Brat? Bitch? All or any of the above?"

Lana snorted with ill-timed laughter but simply shook her head. She bit into her lower lip until her eyes stung.

"Look, I know you've got secrets, we all do. But if you do need a friend, I'd be honored to be there for you. If you need to confide in someone else, do it. Because you're doing yourself no good stressing out like this."

"You're right about that." Lana gave Catharine a weak smile and hoped her gratitude showed.

With a final pat on the back, Catharine started for the door. "I'll hold your calls for an hour or so. Go out, grab a cup of coffee, call a dwarf. Then come back and do the stellar job you always do."

Catharine already had her hand on the doorknob when Lana spoke again. "I'll answer my phone from now on. And thank you, Catharine. I can't tell you how much I appreciate—what you said."

"You mean the lecture?" Catharine gave her a cheeky grin. "Anytime, doll. You're my girl." Then she went out, closing the door behind her.

"Lies," Lana muttered. "I'm not her girl. Or anyone's." But even the little she'd let out to Catharine had helped, and it was past time to pull herself together. While she still had a job. She tried to contemplate bracelets with rapt adoration but couldn't keep her mind on them.

Lana picked up her messages and checked her watch. Isabelle would be out to lunch now. Great time to leave a message. Hopefully her tardiness in returning the message would be overlooked. Quickly Lana dialed Isabelle's number and left a voice mail. Done.

Looking at Daniels' number, Lana reached for the phone. After a moment's indecision, she threw the slip of paper into her trash bin. She tried to concentrate on the bracelets. Then she bent over to fish his number out.

She owed him an explanation. And that was an excuse. She just wanted to hear his voice. Lana threw the number away again.

Five minutes later she retrieved his number from the trash. She already had Dom's opinion, but it was now or never. Still, she hesitated before dialing.

"Hello?"

Warmth rushed over her when she heard his voice. "This is Lana Renault."

"Lana!" Daniel sounded thrilled, but the relief in his voice gave way to gravity. "I need to apologize before we say anything else. I shouldn't have called you at work, but I wanted to say good-bye."

Lana closed her eyes. She was too late. "You're leaving?"

"I think it would be best. I keep hoping for something you don't seem to want. I can tell you I'm not a stalker until the cows come home, but then I do something stupid like call you at work. I get the message."

"How did you find me, anyway?"

"Just called every magazine in Paris and asked for the most beautiful creature in the world."

Lana managed a laugh. "And then what happened when that didn't work?"

"I asked if anyone named Lana worked there. You were the only one."

She should tell Daniel to have a good trip, wherever he was going, and hang up. The thing would be settled and she could get back to work.

"So I guess this is good-bye," Daniel said. "To my regret."

Dom was completely right: she knew next to nothing about Daniel. Why couldn't she say good-bye and hang up?

"Are you still there?"

"I don't want you to go," Lana gasped out.

"This isn't an ultimatum. I didn't call to pressure you. I can go away for a few months and give you some space if you want to think about it. I still feel like we have something special together, and I guarantee I won't change my mind about that. When I come back, if you don't want to see me… I won't bother you again."

"Daniel, there is something I must tell you."

"Yes, you were about to tell me something at the river."

Her eyes squeezed shut, Lana tapped her forehead with her fist. On the phone, she couldn't see the disappointment or revulsion in his face, but she couldn't bring herself to say the words. "It's hard on the phone."

"You're married to a wrestler with a twenty-inch neck and you have eleven children waiting at home for you?"

Way to break the ice. She giggled. "No, of course not."

"As long as you're not cheating on someone, I don't see the problem."

But she was cheating Daniel. Now was the moment, but Lana found it no easier to work out a way to tell him. "That's not it either."

Daniel's voice was persuasive. "If you think I would stop wanting to see you, maybe you shouldn't tell me, because I don't want to stop. Seeing you, that is."

"I just can't say it over the phone."

"What if we meet again and have a good time? Give me another chance to impress you before you dump me. Maybe I can convince you to trust me with whatever it is."

"I don't know if that's a good idea."

"Which is it to be? Will you meet me again, or are we only strangers who almost shared one kiss on the banks of the Seine?"

"Are you always this persistent?"

"No one's ever mattered this much before. I think that's why I made so many mistakes. I was afraid of losing you."

Lana decided to own what she wanted. The release of tension left her feeling light and decisive. "I would like to see you again."

"Tonight?"

She needed a chance to shave her legs. "What about tomorrow?"

"Shall I pick you up?"

Thinking of the dwarfs, who had taken to dropping around unexpectedly, Lana quickly vetoed that option. "No, I'll meet you. Where are we going?"

"Pretend I'm your fairy godfather." Daniel's voice was filled with relief. "Is there something you've always wanted to do since you came to Paris and never have? Tell me your dreams and I'll try to make them come true."

Perhaps she was so unused to anyone wanting so much to please her that Daniel was hard to resist. "I've always want to go on one of those tour boats on the Seine, but it seems so touristy."

"And what are we? Natives?"

Lana had to laugh. "Fair enough. You have a point."

"It's settled, then. Let's meet tomorrow at Pont Neuf at seven and we shall cruise down the center of Paris in style."

WHEN LANA rushed home after work the next day without calling Dom back, he knew something was up. His anxiety level at an all-time high, he stationed himself near her office building to keep an eye out for her. Hating himself for doing it, he followed her home. Although it hurt damnably that she was avoiding him, Dom knew it wasn't because she was angry. Lana was lonely for something her friends couldn't give her.

Dom would rather have been out with his boyfriend, getting to know him better. Only the memory of the time he'd found Lana in that alley in London kept him to his purpose. Now standing in a doorway near her building, Dom rubbed his eyes as if that could erase the terrible image, and then opened them again in a hurry. He didn't want to miss her when she came out.

All Dom wanted was to protect her, even if he tended to deliver that message in a truculent shout. Imagining her walled up in a tower like Rapunzel and himself climbing her hair gave him a chuckle, but it hadn't worked out so well for the witch. Besides, he had no enchanted tower handy and he had his own life to see to.

If Lana refused to talk about her obvious attraction to Daniel, then Dom was just going to have to take matters into his own hands. And he wasn't above shanghaiing Terry into the project. Working evenings, Colin was off the hook, but if Dom had to suffer, Terry could put his time in too. Besides, Terry had a car and it was raining.

When Terry drove up, Dom glanced up at Lana's window, crossed the street, and slipped into the car.

"Is she still up there?"

"Hasn't come out yet." Dom's answer was terse. Even a doof like Terry should be able to figure out that if Lana had already left, he wouldn't still be standing in the rain.

"You sure she's going to meet him?"

"No, I'm not fucking sure. She's not telling me, is she? I just have a bad feeling about this."

To his surprise, Terry reached over to clasp his shoulder briefly. "You're probably right, Dom, but we can't watch her forever."

"I finally got onto a reporter in New York who knows all about Mr. Daniel Hunter, even the juicy stuff that didn't make it into print. He's going to e-mail me all he has," Dom said. "Tomorrow I'll be able to tell her everything Mr. Hunter has done and hopefully she'll smarten up and give him the boot."

Terry cleared his throat ostentatiously several times, and Dom was getting sick of it. "What's the problem, Terry? Spit it out."

"So tonight's the last night for us to follow her?"

The hope in Terry's voice annoyed Dom. "Is Martine upset?"

"Odd as it may seem, she'd actually enjoy spending a bit of time with me, seeing as we're living together," Terry said. "What about Gilles?"

"He doesn't understand. I can't tell him about Lana without her permission." Dom settled back to watch the rain slide down the windscreen and smear the streetlights into a blur.

Terry cleared his throat again. "Pardon me for saying so if it's not true, but you're freaking out over this Daniel guy so bad you're acting more like a stalker than he is!"

"What are you talking about?" Dom swiveled to stare at him.

"Daniel hasn't shown his face around Lana's flat after that first time, but here we are, sitting in a car like a couple of undercover cops getting ready to follow her. Remember before that first date, we promised to keep out of it, but you suddenly felt compelled to order our driver to pull over and then practically kidnapped Lana off the street. And then, just in case she hadn't thought of the risk herself, which I'm sure she had because she's a smart cookie, you start laying down the law to her about telling this guy—"

"Does it make any sense for her to lie about it? How would that help in the long run? He would find out eventually and then the—"

Terry cut him off. "I'm not talking about her behavior right now. I'm talking about yours."

Dom tried to rub his throbbing temples while still keeping his eyes open in case Lana came out. "I'm only trying to keep her safe."

"Dom, we all want her to be safe, but you're acting like a jailer, not a friend. Maybe it's not smart for her to go out with this guy, but she's an adult. That's why she won't tell you where she's going. You're being a prick!"

"I thought I was acting like a dick." Maybe he was rubbing his temples too hard, because his head hurt.

"What you're doing is worse than a dick. Why are you so involved in Lana's life that you'd screw up your own? Are you in love with her?"

Aghast, Dom goggled at Terry. "Of course I'm not in love with her! Don't be ridiculous."

"So why are we here, Dom? Answer me that or you can get the fuck out of my car and run along behind her on foot on your own."

Dom suddenly slid down in the seat. "Wait. This cab could be for her."

A taxi pulled up in front of Lana's building and honked. A minute later Lana emerged from her building and got in.

As the taxi pulled away, Dom said, "Follow her, Ter. I'm begging. I promise I'll tell you all about it. You'll understand then."

Terry slammed his car into gear. "All right, just this once. You'd better come across or you'll walk home. I don't care if it's pouring cats and dogs."

BECAUSE IT was raining, Lana decided on black trousers with high ankle boots. Checking herself in the mirror, she smoothed the claret silk of her blouse and fussed with a turquoise scarf with silver swirls. Then Lana wrapped herself in an embroidered velvet cape. She settled a fedora carefully on her head so as not to muss up her hair.

When she arrived at Pont Neuf, Daniel was waiting in the middle of the bridge under an umbrella, but his smile was brilliant when she emerged from the cab.

For the first time, Daniel wore a proper suit and tie. Anticipation shone in his eyes. "I thought I'd meet you here in case you could use an arm to lean on going down the stairs in those shoes."

Lana couldn't stop smiling. "Something wrong with four-inch heels?" A sudden thought struck her. "You don't mind that it makes me a little taller than you?"

"You can wear anything you want."

That hit a bit close to the bone and struck Lana silent.

Daniel held the umbrella entirely over her without touching her. "The stairs are a little steep."

"I'll be fine." The railing was wet and soaked into her glove, but Lana hung on to it for support. She wished she had taken Daniel's arm when she saw other couples clinging together under their umbrellas. Droplets of rain shone in his hair, but he didn't seem to notice. Lana slipped her hand into the crook of his elbow and moved closer, so the umbrella shielded both of them.

When they reached the landing at the bottom, Daniel led the way to an old-fashioned wooden boat.

Lana didn't want to show how charming she found both him and the boat, but inside she was a sucker for it. "Isn't it a bit wet and chilly for this?"

"The boat is enclosed and heated." Daniel took Lana's elbow to steady her as they walked up the gangplank.

A man with a clipboard stood under a canopy and he nodded at Daniel in recognition. "S'il vous plaît, monsieur." He guided them onto the boat and directly to a private table at the bow of the top deck.

Impressed, Lana looked back over her shoulder as Daniel helped her with her cape. "How did you arrange this?"

"No magic involved. I made a reservation."

Finally Lana couldn't hide her enthusiasm any longer. "This is so lovely. Not at all like those big, crowded tourist boats."

"And there are even some natives aboard, in case you're worried about our credibility." Daniel sat down next to her. "In the meantime,

I wanted to get your approval on these." Daniel pulled up the leg of his trousers to show off his socks.

Lana burst out laughing. "Very original. 'Kapow' and 'Blam' woven inside yellow starbursts against a bright red sock with black polka dots?"

"Missed one." Daniel pointed to one of the bursts.

"Love?" Lana's voice cracked on the word.

"Not quite what you had in mind?"

"I've never even seen such… um… unique footwear."

"Very tactfully put, but I really didn't plan to embarrass you." He pulled down the red cartoon socks, revealing a tasteful dark navy sock with a repeating pattern of slim aqua and purple diamonds up the sides. "I can take them off if you prefer."

"I'm oddly touched, but I like them. Maybe I forgot to say that fashion can also be fun."

"I made you laugh."

"If that was your goal, you succeeded."

Daniel laughed. He had nice teeth. "Have I ever told you how pretty you look when you laugh?"

"No, but I have a mirror."

"You're supposed to say, 'Tell me more.'"

"Tell me more."

"Don't worry, I will. The problem will be getting me to stop."

Nervous again, Lana looked out the window. "The view is breathtaking."

Daniel looked straight at Lana when he agreed. "Yes, it is."

A thrill tiptoed up Lana's spine, although she steeled herself not to show it. From his expression, Lana could have sworn that he knew and it didn't matter. But there was no possible way Daniel could know. She had to get her imagination under control. She could not possibly be in love with Daniel after one and one-quarter dates and a phone call. The novelty of being out with a man was going to her head. Now Lana regretted not letting Dom know about this date, but at least they were in a public place, and Daniel could hardly be planning to murder her and toss her body overboard with so many witnesses aboard.

The smooth action of the boat pulling away from the pier was barely perceptible except as the scenery shifted away from them. Their waiter brought wine and the first course. The food was delicious.

"Looks like the rain is stopping."

"We'll have a good view after all," Lana said. "Oh look, the underside of the bridge is all lit up!"

"I thought this might be fun," Daniel said.

"It's wonderful." Looking at the other couples on board, Lana could have sworn they were all in love. The way Daniel smiled at her, they looked like every other couple on board, but appearances were deceiving. And she was the one doing the deceiving. Lana shook off her doubts. She wanted to enjoy the moment, especially as it might be their last. "It's lovely to see all the familiar sights of Paris from the boat."

"A different perspective?" Daniel's smile seemed almost too understanding.

Lana looked away from him quickly and pointed. "Le Jardin des Tuileries."

Daniel gave it a quick glance. "Looks like a black hole. Must look better by day."

"Well, it is a garden."

The boat went around a bend in the river to reveal the top of the Eiffel Tower poking up above the trees. It was already lit up against the dark blue sky. As they moved past the screen of the trees, the sparkling light show started, bulbs flickering up and down the Tower as they floated by.

"How beautiful!" Lana exclaimed. "The Tower looks so lovely from the river with all those lights dancing in the water."

"Yes."

Something in Daniel's voice made Lana turn to look at him.

"All my life, I wondered how one woman could be so bewitching it was worth launching a thousand ships to get her back. And then I found out when I met you."

Tossing caution overboard, Lana impulsively reached out to touch his hand. "Well, at least I launched one boat."

"Did you never have a dream?" Daniel asked. "Something you wished for more than anything in your life?"

Lana drew her hand back. "It doesn't pay to dream. They never come true."

"I think mine is." Daniel toyed with his wineglass. "I want to make yours come true too."

"Please, Daniel…." She needed desperately to tell him, but this was not the right time. The thought of an emotional scene here horrified her. "I was wrong to agree to this."

"I'm glad you came, Lana. Relax. I won't ask for anything you don't want to give. I enjoy being with you, and I hoped you enjoyed my company too."

"I do," Lana admitted, "but—"

"No buts tonight."

Distracted from her plan to confess, Lana giggled so hard she snorted. "Sorry. I have the sense of humor of a twelve-year-old."

Daniel grinned. "So do I. We're a perfect match. Let's just enjoy the rest of the cruise. I won't say any more right now. We have plenty of time to reveal all our secrets later. I haven't forgotten that you have something to tell me."

"All right." Lana smiled back at him. "I suppose I have nowhere to run at any rate."

"GREAT WAY to spend an evening. We sit here and starve while they have a Colin-worthy dinner on a boat where we can't see them," Terry griped. "Brilliant planning. I'm hungry."

"I am too."

"I don't care if you are. You knew we were going to play MI5 agents tonight, so it was up to you to bring food along."

"I'm sorry, all right?"

"You are a sorry excuse for a friend. And if you're not going to feed me, you better start talking and right now. You're stalling about why you're acting like a dick."

"I'm not stalling. Exactly. Okay. Remember when Lana ended up in hospital that time?"

"When we were fifteen? Yeah."

"Well, I found her."

"I know, you told us."

Dom punched Terry in the arm. "I *found* her, you asshole. She was covered in blood, man. I just—" He covered his face with his hands. Dom felt Terry's hand grip his shoulder briefly.

"Maybe it's past time for you to get this off your chest. Why didn't you tell us the whole story then?"

Dom let his hands fall into his lap and stared at them. "Guess I was trying to protect you guys. And Lana doesn't like hearing about it, so I try not to remind her."

"Does she remember what happened?"

"Not all of it. The docs said some of it might never come back. And I sure as hell hope it doesn't."

"So what did happen?"

"You and Colin were away on that school outing my parents thought was rubbish. Remember Lana was living on the streets by then. I used to smuggle part of my breakfast out of the house and bring it to her in the morning."

"And Lana could always put away a lot."

"Maybe she eats like that now because she was practically starving when she was on the streets. I just wanted to take care of her. We used to meet on Greenbriar Street by the bus stop. I got there that morning and no Lana."

"Well it's not like she had an alarm clock or anything." Terry shifted in his seat.

"She was always on time, so I got worried. I didn't want to miss her, but I also didn't want to be late to school and get into trouble. So I finally went looking in all the places I knew she hung out. Nothing.

Not a sight of her." Dom began to pant. "You know where the George and Dragon pub is, and that little alley next to it?"

Terry nodded.

"I—I went down there because sometimes they'd give her a handout round the back. I saw a bundle of rags by the skip. As I got closer, I noticed some red spray paint on the wall. The garbage reeked, but there was another smell, kind of metallic. I—I was scared as hell, but I kept walking forward like I was in a trance or something.

"Then I saw the rags were moving. I saw her *hair* on the ground—he'd cut most of it off. It was all over the pavement, but I recognized the color and the curls. I crouched down and I touched her shoulder—by then I realized it was a person, I mean Lana, but I was hoping it wasn't her, but if it was I couldn't let her just lie there even if she was—dead. I rolled her on her back and I heard a gurgling noise.

"Her face, ahh, her face—" Dom squeezed his eyes shut, as if that could erase the sight. "It was shiny—glistening—with blood. Lying on her back, she started choking on the blood, so I rolled her onto her side. And then I realized—that red paint was her *blood*. I ran. I beat on the door of the pub, but it was closed. I just kept pounding on doors until someone opened up. I told them to call the police and I ran back, hoping she wasn't gone yet."

"Dom… my God!"

"Then I sat down next to her and held her hand. Her hand, Terry, it was black with dried blood and bruises, but it was still warm. And I just kept talking to her, telling her I had her breakfast and begging her not to die on me—gahh!" Dom couldn't help choking out a sob, and then, embarrassed, he wiped his eyes.

Terry reached over and gripped Dom's shoulder hard. "I'm so sorry—for both of you."

Overwhelmed by guilt, Dom could take no comfort from his friend's touch. "They took her to hospital and the police took me to school after I told them who she was and gave them her parents' number and all. They asked how I recognized her. She was wearing that stupid purple dress with the flowers. Remember how she loved that rag? It was that and her hair. And I kept thinking how mad she was going to be when she woke up and found the bastard had cut it off. She'd only just managed to grow it long enough to touch her shoulders, but what if she never woke up? I guess her hair wouldn't have mattered then, but she would have been so upset." He realized he was barely making sense and took a deep breath to stem the tide of words.

"How did you manage to stay in school all day, Dom?"

"No problem there. I spent the day in the nurse's office. Barfing. As soon as school let out, I snuck over to the hospital. Must have walked miles of hallways trying to find Lana, because I figured they wouldn't tell me. They'd cleaned the blood off her by then. She was asleep or unconscious. They had her on a respirator, and the part of her face I could see was so swollen and bloody and beat up, I couldn't even recognize her. The name tag on the door was the only clue I was in the right room. Big ruddy bandage around her neck where he cut her throat. And her hair was just tufts sticking out all over." The memory made him shudder, and Terry's fingers tightened on his shoulder.

"She is *definitely* a fighter. Defensive wounds all over her arms. She fought to stay alive just like she fought to wear her dresses."

"Dom, I'm really sorry I handed you a bunch of shit earlier, but why didn't you tell us at the time, man?" Terry gave his shoulder a shake. "You know Col and I never thought it—"

"I know, but I didn't want to lay it on you guys. It's not something I like dwelling on, and I don't like to remind her. I felt so guilty she was out there on her own."

"Don't be silly, Dom. What could you do? You were just a kid yourself."

"I keep trying to tell myself that, but maybe I could have snuck her into—"

"It's over and done, Dom. Did they catch the guy?"

"Yeah. He still had the knife on him. Lana's parents agreed to a plea bargain so there was no trial. The most important thing to dear old Dad was making sure the media didn't get hold of it. It would never do for the public to find out they had a son who liked to dress like a girl and some nut tried to rape her and then cut her up when he found out she was really a boy."

"How about being embarrassed their child would rather live on the streets instead of with them?" Terry slammed his hand against the dash, and Dom jumped at the sound.

"Come on, Ter. You've met them. When did they ever give a fuck about their demon child?"

"Listen, Dom, I get what you're saying, and clearly you're still suffering from the shock of finding Lana that way, but you're still being a dick following her around."

"Who are you and where is my friend Dopey?" Dom laughed nervously, but Terry didn't give him even a flicker of a smile.

Terry plowed right past his lame quip. "Dom, I may play the dumb blond to put my clients at ease, but you know me better than that. You are pushing it with Lana. You're skirting damn close to victimizing her yourself and then justifying it in the name of keeping her safe."

"I know, I know. I can't seem to help it. I start reliving that panic and I can't bear to let Lana out of my sight. It's been difficult enough to explain all this to Gilles. He probably thinks I'm two-timing him, but don't you see? Any time a man asks her out, she's got to either say no or find some way to tell them a fact about herself that makes a lot of men see red. They get mad either way! Hell, just last week some poor girl in the US was shot because she refused to give her number to a stranger in a bar. How do we know Daniel isn't a psycho who'll pull a knife on Lana again? Or maybe it'll be a gun this time."

"I see your point and yet—"

"She asked me to help her find a way to tell Daniel, and I was working on it, but there's really no good way except to stand out of reach in a public place with plenty of witnesses around and hope

106

for the best. There's something about this fellow Daniel that rubs me the wrong way. Let's hope we put an end to the entire thing tomorrow."

"Consider this, Dom. Is there any man at all you could tolerate getting close to Lana who wouldn't rub you the wrong way? Forgive me for saying so, but you just told me a pretty harrowing story, and it's clear you're not over it yet. Perhaps your judgment about Daniel might be just a bit skewed, wouldn't you say?"

"You may be right, Terry. But I'm still going to tell Lana anything I find out about Mr. Hunter. At least she'll know."

"Even if she never speaks to us again."

"That's what I'm most afraid of." Dom stared out the rain-streaked windscreen. Without any other solution, he had to follow his chosen course of action.

Terry broke the long silence. "The guy in the alley. He didn't cut off her, um, penis, did he?"

A sharp bark of laughter escaped Dom, and then he laughed again at the shock on Terry's face. "No, Ter. Don't know how he missed doing that, but the family jewels are intact. Thanks for asking, though."

"This whole thing is going to give me nightmares as it is," Terry muttered. "I'm glad she's still whole."

"Yeah, nightmares. Welcome to my world."

"At least now I know why you're so obsessive about her."

"Well, there's that and also I really am kind of a dick. You have to be in journalism." Dom grinned at Terry, feeling lighter already. Confession must be good for the soul, and sharing the weight seemed to lessen the burden. Terry might have nightmares tonight, but Dom was pretty sure he wouldn't for once.

WHEN THE boat returned to the dock, the rain had vanished into fog. The streetlamps had turned into romantic, misty globes shining through the gray night.

"Did you enjoy the boat ride?"

"It was magical," Lana murmured. "I wish it could go on...."

"The night doesn't have to end yet." Daniel held out his hand. "Shall we walk beside the river again?"

Looking at the other couples strolling along and aching to be like them, Lana took Daniel's hand, even though she should resist temptation. This had already gone further than she'd ever intended, but it felt so good just holding hands. "I shouldn't stay out too late."

"Ah yes, the pumpkin coach might roll up any second, but let's enjoy the few moments of freedom we have left."

Dom's words of caution echoed in Lana's brain. No need for Daniel to know she'd given the dwarfs the slip. Although the way Daniel looked at her....

She either told Daniel the truth now or that they couldn't meet again. In fact, it was probably already too late, and that was her fault. She owed Daniel the truth, if nothing else.

Lana dropped Daniel's hand and took a few steps back, groping in her bag to find the pepper spray. She pulled the container out and held it so tight her fingers felt as if they would never straighten out again.

"Daniel, I have something I must tell you."

"That you love me and want to spend the rest of your life with me?" Daniel flicked a glance at Lana's hand, but he was still smiling at her. Maybe the spray didn't register. "Or at least tonight?"

"Please be serious."

Daniel stopped smiling. "I'm sorry. Tell me anything you want, Lana."

"Daniel, my name is Roland." Lana waited for the explosion. Ready to run if necessary, every muscle rigid with tension, Lana could barely catch her breath. Her knuckles were white as she gripped the canister hard, index finger on the button, waiting for anger, revulsion—even violence. "I'm not a girl."

After a short silence, Daniel said, "I know. I was waiting for you to tell me."

"How did you know? How could you?" Terror and fury throbbed in her veins. That was the last thing she'd expected to hear. Daniel remained oddly calm.

"Artists sometimes see things that other people miss." Daniel stretched out a hand but let it fall when Lana moved out of reach. "And if it's any consolation, I wasn't sure right away. You are a beautiful woman."

Lana waited to see whether Daniel would examine her face as other men had, searching for traces of maleness under the makeup. Instead Daniel looked into Lana's eyes. Although his body mirrored her tension, he stayed at a safe distance.

Still wary, Lana rotated her head to loosen her neck muscles. "Why are you after me? What do you want? I don't have any money."

"There's nothing to blackmail you about in my opinion. I'm not after your money, I have plenty." The shock on his face convinced Lana he was telling the truth. "The moment I saw your face I knew you were the one for me. And I'm the one for you."

"How romantic." She finally heard the words she'd longed for and Lana could not believe they were true. She couldn't hold back her sneer. "Love at first sight, is that it? Except the princess turns out to be a frog."

"Then let me kiss you and break the spell." Daniel took a tiny step closer.

"Don't touch me." Lana raised the pepper spray and backed away.

He stood completely still, hands raised. "Can't you believe that I could want you anyway?"

"So far when men have found out I don't have the 'right parts,' they've taken it as a personal insult." Lana's voice cracked, and she tried again. "One that requires they avenge their manhood."

Anger flashed in Daniel's eyes. "Then they aren't real men. Who you are doesn't define their masculinity."

"You're probably right, but unfortunately the result tends to be harder on me than it is on them."

Daniel curled his hands into fists. "I wish I could hunt down everyone who ever hurt you and kick their butts for you, Lana."

"Excellent. I'll send you a list."

"I know it's asking a lot, but please give me a chance."

"The chance would be more on my side, wouldn't it?"

"I know you have no reason to trust me—"

"No reason at all."

"We've had fun together. We laughed. We're made for each—"

"I am not made for anyone." Lana took a step back when she really wanted to move forward. If she'd never gone out with Daniel in the first place, she wouldn't be in this fix now.

Daniel's shoulders rose and then slumped in defeat. "It seems the only way to prove my sincerity is to walk away. That's the kind of irony I usually appreciate, but not when it hurts so damn much."

Lana sank her teeth into her lower lip, still trying to decide whether Daniel was lying.

Daniel waited, but when Lana didn't move or speak, he turned to stare out at the river. "I wish we could have met in a different time, Lana. When things like this didn't matter. Maybe it was too soon." His chin quivered as he looked at the water. "I was wrong to try to be part of your life. I'm sorry." His head bowed, Daniel started back the way they'd come.

Emotion rushed through Lana, and at first she mistook it for relief. Lana thought she'd stopped fantasizing that a happy ending was possible for her, but watching Daniel walk away with his head down like a man who had received a crushing blow, Lana knew she'd been deluding herself. Dominick was definitely right. Getting to know Daniel solved nothing. It only made her want him more. The dream of having someone all to herself seemed to vanish with every step Daniel took.

The broken part inside that Lana had worked so hard to heal shattered again into a million sharp little pieces, each one stabbing deep into her heart. She could almost feel her blood welling up around each tiny pinprick, slowly at first and then turning into a flood of agony. Right now Lana would have given everything—her clothes, her job, even her friends—to have Daniel back again. How could a man she'd seen only three times have become so important to her so quickly?

The fear Lana had wrapped around herself like a shield lied to her. Looking at the rigid line of pain that was Daniel's spine, Lana could remember only the kindness in his eyes, the joy in his smile, and the safe feeling of Daniel holding her hand.

The thought of never seeing him again—

"Daniel, wait!" Lana's throat was dry. She cleared it and tried again. "Daniel…."

Only a croak emerged, but Daniel must have heard it. He stopped dead in his tracks and whirled around.

Her feet like lead, Lana started to run, still holding the pepper spray. Daniel broke into a run also, closing the distance between them.

Breathing hard, Lana held out her hand to keep Daniel at a safe distance. "Wait—I have to tell you I've had to—leave where I was living several times. I decided—I simply won't take a chance anymore. Paris feels like home, and I don't want to leave here just because—"

"I'll leave you alone if that's what you wish, but I hope that's not what you're saying. Please tell me you've changed your mind." The light from the streetlamps illuminated the yearning in Daniel's eyes.

Lana needed to be certain of what Daniel was after. "I—I can see you desire me, but are you looking for an exotic, freaky sex show, or is it the person you want? I have two arms, two legs, and an adequate number of holes, so sex wouldn't be much different than with anyone else."

"I won't deny that I'm attracted to your appearance, Lana, but for us, sex will be different. We'll be making love."

Lana gave a bitter laugh. "Because we're so special? And what makes it different for us?"

Daniel took a step forward and stopped when Lana backed up again. "How can I convince you? You make me feel so fucking alive. When you laugh, you light up a dark space deep inside me. I make a fool of myself to get you to smile so I can see the stars in your eyes. It's not how you look or what you wear, it's how I feel when I'm with you. And I hope that's how you feel when you're with me."

"I won't change who I am for anyone." Lana's voice came out firmer than she actually felt.

"I haven't asked you to. I want to get to know you. I want to undress you and ravish you with pleasure. I—I can't even believe I'm saying this, but I want to make you love me." Daniel stretched out a hand toward Lana. "I don't know how to ask this gracefully, but are you a girl now?"

Lana flinched from Daniel's touch. "The original plumbing is still intact."

Quickly, Daniel dropped his hand. "I'm sorry, I offended you. I didn't mean to pry."

Despite the awkwardness, Lana had to giggle. "Well, I suppose if we did end up in bed, you have a right to know what to look forward to."

When Lana laughed, the rigidity left Daniel's shoulders. "I only meant, do you consider yourself a she... or a he?"

"Do I have to choose? Wear a label to make it easier on everyone else? I just want to be me. I don't need to define myself that way."

"I'm sorry. That's not what I meant either. You can be whoever you want. I'll just trail along behind holding up your train so it doesn't drag through the mud."

That made Lana giggle. "Fabulous! The last footman couldn't be trusted, and one of my trains was never the same."

"I hope to give satisfaction." Daniel's smile faded. He drew his brows together. "I'm trying to get this right. Just tell me how you wish to be referred to. I'm guessing she?"

"That is what I prefer." He was actually asking what she preferred!

Daniel came closer. "May I hold your hand?"

Lana nodded, unable to speak. She finally relaxed her grip on the pepper spray and dropped it into her purse.

Gently Daniel took both Lana's hands and held them pressed flat against his chest. "I don't want to mess up Paris for you. You were here first. If you tell me to, I'll leave. I can go to Rome or London or Madrid. Just tell me what you want."

Hard as it was to claim her desire, somehow Lana managed to say it out loud. "I want you to stay." The rapid thump of Daniel's heart against her palms seemed to beat in time to her own bounding pulse.

Daniel's face lit up with joy. "Does this mean I have a chance?"

"This feels like *I* have a chance—it feels almost like coming out again, but better. How did you—when did you know?"

"I couldn't pinpoint the difference at first."

Light dawned. "You used *beau* instead of *belle* the first time we talked."

Daniel grinned. "And you ignored it. Then when we met the second time at Henri's, I knew for sure."

"And you asked me out anyway?" Her voice was soft with wonder.

"I asked you out anyway, and I had a wonderful time. The envy of every man who saw us. Don't worry, most people would never notice, but you don't have to hide from me."

Lana smiled up at him. "Maybe we both have a chance."

"Your hands are cold. Let's get some coffee." Daniel smiled reassuringly. "We'll take it slow."

"THERE, SHE told him, see? And he doesn't look as though he's planning to kill her." Terry pointed through the windscreen.

Dom groaned aloud at the sight of Daniel holding Lana. "That reporter better come through in the morning."

"It wasn't bad enough when they got on that damn boat and we had to sit here for two solid hours wondering what the hell they were doing." Terry looked at his watch. "I strongly advise against swooping in and kidnapping her again. Not if you want to stay friends with her. Or me. We're not using my car for that."

Exhausted, Dom slumped in his seat. "We're her only friends. We should at least see she gets home all right."

"Because we don't trust her?"

"We don't trust him."

"They're getting into a taxi. We're in for it now," Terry said gloomily.

"I know she's lonely," Dom said. "But we ought to be enough for her!"

"Of all the arrogant…," Terry snapped. "That's why Colin and I have girlfriends, right? And why you're dating Gilles."

"We Musketeers should be good enough for one another." Weak. As if he was trying to convince himself, not Terry.

"You don't touch my musket and I won't touch yours," Terry said. "The point is—"

"The point is we need to see this Daniel guy and let him know we know all about him. And then we've got to tell *her*."

"I'm going to say this again. It's tragic and unfair that something so shocking happened to both of you," Terry started.

"It happened to Lana, not me."

"You were only fifteen, and no one expects to find their friend that way."

"Right, and your point is?"

"You think you're trying to find out all about him and tell Lana so she'll dump him. But it sounds as if you don't care how much you hurt her in the process as long as you're comfortable with it. Colin and I always wondered what happened to you guys that year. Well, now we know: you were both traumatized in a horrible way. I don't trust your judgment on this. We're going to see Colin in the morning and tell him the whole story. Then, because we're Musketeers, one for all and all for one, we'll take a vote on whether we meddle in her business like that. And by we, I mean you."

"Let's see where they're going," Dom ordered. "Follow that cab."

Terry just stared at him. "No."

"We have to keep her safe!"

Terry put his head down on the steering wheel and breathed heavily. "Dammit." Then he turned on the engine. "I'm doing this for you, Dom, not Lana."

CHAPTER 8

WHEN SHE heard the knock on her door the next morning, for a moment Lana thought it might be him. But Daniel still didn't know where she lived. After their coffee, she had allowed Daniel to find her a cab and she went home alone.

Lana ran a fingertip back and forth over her lips, wishing she could recapture the sensation of his mouth on hers. Daniel had kissed her, knowing what she was. Just a brush of the lips and the world tilted off its axis and the stars realigned in the heavens. She had dreamed of it all night. Or had she really slept at all?

The knock sounded again, louder this time. Lana roused herself, put on her dressing gown, went to the door, and opened it. Dom was frowning.

Resigned, Lana stepped back to allow him to enter. "Bonjour, Happy. I'll make coffee."

"Stop calling me that!" Dom ordered. "Late night?"

The miniscule kitchen, consisting of a sink and two burners, was squeezed into a niche. A tiny refrigerator nestled under the stainless steel countertop. Lana got busy grinding the coffee beans. "You ought to know. You were there."

"You saw us?"

"You're pretty good, but it probably wasn't wise to use Dopey's car. I know his license plate."

"Speaking of stuff you ought to know," Dom started in grim triumph, "I've been doing a little research on Mr. Daniel Hunter. He's not safe for you to know."

"And how do you know that?" Lana turned on him.

"Did you not just hear me? I looked him up. He's got quite a shady past."

"So do I, if you want to get technical." Lana winced at the edge in her voice, but her sarcasm didn't seem to deter Dom. Her buoyant mood melted away in the face of Dom's words.

"But you're *our* friend. Let his friends look out for him, if he has any. We don't care if you hurt him, only if he hurts you."

"He knows about me," Lana said. "I told him. He won't hurt me."

"He's a con man, Lana."

The rush of disappointment revealed just how much she'd hoped that Daniel was telling the truth. She couldn't let even Dom see how much this hurt. And Dom *was* hurting her, for God's sake, implying that no one would ever want her for her.

"Didn't you hear me, Lana? That's his gig. Get a rich woman to trust him and then take her for all she's got."

"So he'll learn not to fuck with a working girl. We have a lot less to lose." Lana forced a smile. Her face hurt with the effort. She waved a hand to indicate the tiny kitchen. "I don't have enough money to make blackmail a worthwhile risk."

"Your family has a lot more to lose."

Stunned, Lana stared at Dom. "He doesn't know about them. I changed my name, remember? There's no link between us."

"Don't be naive. I bet I could track you down on the Internet and make the connection, and if I could, he could too. He probably found out all about you before he asked you out. Why else would he keep coming after you like he did?"

Lana slammed her hand on the counter. "Did it ever occur to you he might actually like me? He wouldn't get a shilling from my family. If he sent a ransom letter and threatened to dispose of me, they'd probably write back and thank him."

"But what if he threatened to publicize who you are now and who you were. Your family would pay to prevent that little scandal, wouldn't they?"

The roaring in her ears somehow couldn't prevent Dom's words from sinking in.

"Your father, the MP, is trying to make gay marriage illegal in Britain again, and his career is very important to him."

"I know. I saw him on TV. But he doesn't know where I am."

"But Daniel does. How's it going to make MP Reynolds look if voters found out his own son is gay? And not only gay, you like to dress like a woman. When you were attacked, he jumped at the chance to unload a liability. Ever wonder why he allowed you to change your name?"

"I knew he didn't want anyone to know we were related, but hell, neither did I," Lana said.

"When you were in hospital, dear old Dad held a press conference to announce that you were murdered by a pervert homosexual out to seduce children to the dark side. Barrett Reynolds built his entire career on your supposed death. Whenever anyone slightly left of center looked as if they were gaining ground, why he could just trot out the ghost of his son Roland, martyred in the great crusade to keep Britain white and pure and heterosexual, and whip up some handy outrage.

"Don't you think if Hunter showed up and threatened to reveal where the press could find his son, who dresses and lives like a woman, that it would be worth the money to MP Reynolds to make sure you never show up to embarrass him again?"

Lana closed her eyes to prevent tears from spilling over. She would not allow Dom to see her cry. "I can't believe Daniel would do that." Dom touched her arm, but she recoiled.

"You don't want to believe. I just told you that Daniel has a history as a blackmailer, so this isn't a big reach for him, but it could be a big payoff. Finish the coffee—"

She opened her eyes and screamed at him. "I don't want any coffee!"

"Neither do I! I care about you, Lana, and I'm not going to let anyone hurt you."

"Except you!" She opened and closed her hands like cat's claws.

"This might cost our friendship, but we need to confront Daniel and get the truth. You need to hear his story from him. Colin and Terry are holding Mr. Daniel Hunter at his place. We're going over to get all this out in the open."

"You don't have the right to fling orders at me!" Lana exclaimed.

"Lana, I'm afraid for you. No, scratch that. *Terrified* for you. I don't want you to hate me, but if you don't face this now, you'll always wonder. Maybe you and Daniel have a future, but you can't build it on lies and secrets."

"I'm trying not to hate you right now, and I'm not succeeding." Lana realized Dom's lower lip was trembling. "I know you're doing this… because you want to protect me, but I…."

"I hope for your sake that I'm wrong, Lana. Really I do. But how can we find out if we don't confront him?"

GRAY CLOUDS looming low over the city were a perfect match for her mood. The only thing missing was rain. No matter how Dom tried to rouse her, Lana stayed silent for the entire walk to Daniel's flat. Until the threat of having it all taken away, Lana hadn't realized exactly how much she'd invested in a virtual stranger. And here she'd thought she was being careful. An inappropriate snort of laughter took her by surprise, and she gave Dom a dirty look when he dared to look questioningly at her.

She knew the dwarfs were trying to protect her, but right now Lana hated them all. If Daniel turned out to be as bad as they claimed, Lana would have to be more messed up than even she thought to keep wanting him, but she hoped Dom was wrong.

"This is it." Dom turned at the entrance of a building that looked like an old warehouse.

Lana followed him inside and up the curved staircase. Her knees were shaking so badly she had to hang on to the banister to manage the climb.

Dom knocked on a door painted blue. Terry opened the door, a walking stick clutched in his hand, looking far more ferocious than Lana had ever seen him.

"Oh, hi. It's you." Terry lost the scowl and welcomed them inside as if they were there to view the property.

This was not the way she'd hoped to see Daniel's flat for the first time. Lana was curious to see what the place revealed about him that she'd missed. With Dom bringing up the rear, Lana followed Terry into a huge room filled with light streaming in from tall industrial windows. The white plaster ceiling was crossed with aged wooden beams. A couch with modern lines stood on a vast rug in front of the fireplace. The glass coffee table was low and sleek, with several art books stacked neatly upon it. Floating bookshelves on either side of the fireplace displayed books and a few small sculptures.

Lana rotated slowly to take in the room, and then stopped short when she caught sight of a large painting hanging on the wall opposite the fireplace. On a shelf under the painting was a potted orchid with white flowers. Although the painting was framed, the brushstrokes had a sketchy, unfinished feel, as if the artist had tried to capture an impression gathered in an instant. A swirl of color and light depicted a busy Paris street. A girl looked back over her shoulder at the artist, her eyes wide and startled. The wind had caught her hair, partially obscuring her face. The blurred crowd around her was merely blocked in. Daniel's name was scrawled in the lower right-hand corner.

She realized she was looking at her own face. To see herself through Daniel's eyes was a revelation. Every brushstroke seemed to express love. If Daniel was in this just for the con, he could never have painted that picture.

Lana saw a self she'd never seen in the mirror. The guarded look was gone. Although she had secrets to conceal, her eyes were lit with certainty and expectation, as if something wonderful just out of sight was about to appear. The man who could see and understand her so well couldn't want to hurt her.

Out of the corner of her eye, Lana watched Dom's reaction to the painting. He was mesmerized and stared as if he saw what she did. Almost baffled, he shook his head slightly, but his face lost a bit of that bullish determination.

Lana didn't want to give away how much the painting moved her. "Where is he?" She barely managed to get the words out of her tight throat.

Terry pointed at the spiral staircase. "Colin's got him upstairs in the studio. Top floor."

Stalling, Lana took a couple of deep breaths. "This place is so big, you could fit six of my flats in here."

"He's taken the top three floors here," Terry said. "Fabulous view from the studio on the top floor, and on the second a huge bedroom with a view of—"

Dom rolled his eyes. "Will you shut up and focus?"

Terry gave Lana a sly grin. "Three bathrooms."

"A tub?" Lana whispered.

"A big old claw-foot in the one off the hallway." Terry raised his brows. "It's quite a—"

Dom punched Terry in the arm. "Dopey, you don't have to prove you're an idiot every time you open your mouth. You're not showing a property to a pair of prospective buyers here, remember? This is serious."

Terry's smile disappeared. "Sorry, Dom."

"Let's get on with it." Dom led the way up the stairs.

The top floor was one open space with shelves crowded with paints and brushes. A covered easel stood by the north window, and other canvases were stacked neatly against the walls.

Lana almost laughed when she saw the hostage sitting on a worn velvet couch planted at one end of the room, his feet up on a coffee table as he flipped through a magazine. Looking rather outmatched, plump little Colin sat at the opposite end with his arms crossed over his chest, watching Daniel like a hungry hawk.

When he heard them enter, Daniel dropped the magazine and stood up. A vein throbbed in his neck. Lana took an involuntary step toward him and then jerked away.

Dom took Lana's arm. "Not so fast."

"Lana."

Just one word, and her palms were sweating and her pulse beat fast.

EVEN WITH her hair pulled back in a ponytail and her face bare of makeup, Lana was luminous. He'd never seen her in sneakers instead of heels, but the familiar scarf around her throat provided a burst of color to the funereal outfit.

Daniel wished he could hold Lana one last time before he confessed. Even now, when her eyes burned into his as if she'd never seen him before, how could the dwarfs deny the electricity that crackled through the air between them?

Time for Daniel to pay the piper. "After what I have to say, you'll probably never want to speak to me again, but you shared your secret with me. It's only fair I should tell you mine."

Lana's face shut down. She stared at all four men as if they were strangers.

No turning back now. "I need to get this off my chest anyway. I didn't want to hide anything from you. They want me to tell you—"

"How you earned your living off of rich married women and then blackmailing them when the affair was over, Mr. Daniel Hunter." Dom's voice was quiet, in triumph or trepidation. Daniel didn't know which. "Tell her how good you are at making women fall in love with you."

Lana waited in icy silence.

"It's true—" Daniel's voice broke when Lana covered her face with both hands. "It's true I was a con artist for a while. I wasn't a particularly good man back then, but I've—"

"Just your everyday, garden-variety con man who belongs in jail," Colin said.

"Yes, I admit I was a con man, but I'm not the same man now that I was then." Daniel hoped he could make her understand.

"We went down to the river, baptized our sins away, oh, all in the naaaaaaaame of the Loooooooooord," Colin warbled.

"So Danny-boy, you got religion, reformed, returned all the money, and never jaywalked again a day in your life. And there really are fairies." Dom gave Terry a fierce side-eye when he snickered. "Shut up. You know what I mean!"

"I know it sounds like a fairy tale, but I really have changed," Daniel insisted.

"And what brought on this dramatic change?" Dom went on questioning him. Lana still hadn't said a word.

"I almost died." The words dropped like a rock into a pond and spread ripples of silence.

"You have to—to look at life differently after something like that." Daniel laid a hand over his pounding heart.

"I know that." For the first time, Lana spoke, but in a murmur.

Daniel sat down, his elbows on his thighs, head in his hands. Lana crossed the room to the windows and stared outside at the rooftops. If she'd only given him a quick glance, Daniel would have had more hope.

"I'm an artist. It's not a high-paying profession, but eventually I made a name for myself painting portraits."

Dom made a speed-it-up gesture. "And the other artists were jealous, called you an old-fashioned sellout, but the wealthy bought in."

"One day a client's wife made it clear she wanted more than her portrait painted." Daniel rolled his head to ease the tension in his neck. "I guess my morals were more flexible than they should have been. Easy enough to take a few dollars for an afternoon in the sack. I got to paint and eat. That's all there was to it."

"Not quite all," Dom said. "What about the Montagues?"

Daniel rubbed his eyes in dismay. He was ashamed to talk about what he'd done, especially with the dwarfs listening, but Lana deserved honesty in return for hers. "You know about the Montagues."

"I'm a good researcher, so don't bother trying to minimize." Dom crossed his arms over his chest.

"Mrs. Montague wasn't the first—"

"More like the last." Terry's face twisted with contempt.

"At first I just slept with them. Then I got the idea to earn a little severance package when an affair ended. Just a little good-bye payment to guarantee that I walk away without spilling the beans. Without coming right out and saying so, I got the idea across that their husbands would never hear certain facts from me after we split. The first time was an impulse because—let's just say it was an impulse. But it worked out well for me. It got easier every time, and the women were more than willing to pay up."

"What a guy," Terry said.

"I had an affair with Mrs. Montague. When it was over, I put the squeeze on her, but she was the first one who balked." Daniel flinched when Lana turned to look at him. The disgust on her face lanced through him like an icepick.

"Blackmail is worse than murder. Instead of killing the body, you're killing hope." Lana turned away from him to stare out the window again.

Daniel hung his head in shame.

"Then what happened?" Dom prodded.

"It got complicated."

"Complicated how?" Colin asked harshly.

"I called her bluff," Daniel said.

"Mr. Montague was not pleased to learn about the affair," Dom told Lana.

Hating the contempt in their eyes and yet knowing he'd earned it, Daniel soldiered on with his confession. "He called and said his wife told him about my demands and he'd pay."

"Disgusting." The echo of hysteria in Lana's voice made Daniel wince.

She seemed ready to bolt. Daniel put out a hand as if he could stop her, but he didn't dare approach her. Not now, not here. "I *was* disgusting. I'm telling the absolute truth here. I'm not proud of it. I can't even figure—"

"But you took the money from these women." The relentless way Dom pressed for answers gave Daniel a new respect for his abilities.

"Yeah. I did."

"But why?" Lana put her hand to her throat. "Why would you do that to a woman you loved?"

"I never loved any of them!" Daniel pressed his knuckles to his temples to ease the headache. Nothing could ease the ache in his heart. "I liked some of them. I liked the sex, they liked the sex. I did it because I needed the money."

"No empathy for a single one of them?" Lana was skeptical. "Not a hint of remorse?"

"You didn't know them. The money I asked for was nothing to them. I never felt much of anything until I saw—"

"Don't say it." Lana's face contorted with pain and he stopped speaking.

"Go on with Mr. Montague," Dom reminded Daniel.

"Right. Montague was rich and powerful. Used to getting his own way. First he asked about a birthmark that you wouldn't see when she was dressed. Then he set conditions. I had to go to his office to collect. He wanted to see me in person."

"Why?" That was Colin.

Daniel squirmed in embarrassment. "Wanted to compare notes with the guy his wife went to bed with. Even for a tough guy like me, that was pretty hard to take."

"So he paid you after?"

Daniel laughed, although it wasn't funny then or now. "Yeah, but he outsmarted me. I walked in expecting a big score. The way he talked about his wife, I realized when I walked out with the dough, it wouldn't be over for her. Then I started to realize how much damage I'd done. But as soon I had the cash in my hand, three thugs came in and grabbed me. Montague told them to take out the trash. They forced me out the back way into a car. I knew I was in trouble. I was a small-time con artist. I didn't have a gun. Hell, I'd never even been in a fight."

"What happened then?" Dom wasn't showing much mercy.

"They drove me down to the docks to a deserted alley. One of them supervised while the other two kicked the crap out of me. When it was over, I figured I've taken my beating. Win some, lose some. So I'm grunting in pain on the ground. After they leave, I'm lying there trying to figure out how many days it'll take me to make it to my feet, walk out of there, and find a taxi when the supervisor came back for the money. I guess he left with the others because he didn't want a three-way split. Montague didn't even care enough to take it back before he turned me over to the help, that's how small change I was to him. While the thug was searching me, I must have made a sound, because he said, 'I thought you weren't as hurt as you made out.' Then he tried to kill me."

"So how did you get away?" Even Dom was caught up in the story now. He sat down.

Lana had turned around again and was watching Daniel.

"Played dead." Daniel laughed again. "Funny how some people just can't resist a good con. They accused me of conning women, which was absolutely true, and two seconds later the guy believes whatever I say. Although technically I didn't say much of anything. I was too busy bleeding out at the time, so he had some evidence to support the theory that I was dead."

"He shot you?"

"He—he stabbed me." Slowly, Daniel lifted his shirt to reveal two scars on his torso. "Until then, I was always the smart guy. I never let anyone get close enough to hurt me, physically or emotionally."

Lana raised her hand to her throat and swallowed audibly.

126

"Imagine my shock to be the idiot left for dead in some alley, knowing there wasn't a soul on earth who cared if I died." Daniel couldn't help writhing with the shame and humiliation of being a victim. A tide of pain washed over him again, clawing holes in his chest just like the knife had. The visceral fear of that moment still made him feel like puking.

He looked up and found Lana watching him. Her face had changed from disgust to empathy, giving him a wisp of hope to cling to.

Colin broke the moment with a bit of sarcasm. "You look like you work out, Hunter. Why didn't you vanquish the villains before they led you out by the nose?"

"Maybe I should have tried, but it's not a great plan when one guy is holding a gun on you. The irony, which I completely appreciate, is that by almost killing me, they saved my life."

"Explain that," Colin said.

"I had a lot of time to think over my sins while recuperating. I didn't like where I ended up or how I got there. Or who I'd become." Daniel clamped his lips shut. Almost dying held a universal appeal in that everyone was driven to study the misfortune of the victim in hope of avoiding it themselves. His remorse was still too sharp to pour out into the maw of their curiosity. But he had to give them something to chew on.

"Artists are worth more dead than alive. You die, no more paintings, so all your work goes up in price," Daniel explained. "While I was in the hospital, my agent made a killing selling off my work. He rolled the dice and gambled I wouldn't make it. Then he'd get to keep the proceeds for himself."

"That was not very nice," Terry said in a mild tone. Dom rolled his eyes.

Daniel felt like rolling his eyes as well. "Yeah, well, I wasn't exactly holding the moral high ground myself. When I disappointed him by recovering, he had to fork over. I have enough to live on for the rest of my life."

"At first I thought this was the usual, that you would eventually find out about Lana, lose your shit, and try to beat her up." Dom got up and started to pace. "Then I dug into your past and decided you were trying to blackmail her."

"Over what?" Although Daniel had to convince them he was on the level, he really didn't have a clue here.

"Lana's done a good job of creating a new identity, but you could probably find out who her family is and put the screws to her. Or more likely them."

Daniel stared at the floor in defeat. "And I've admitted that's my modus operandi, right? But I never thought of it. I have no idea who her family is. And I have enough money, even if I never paint again. My blackmail career is over."

"Not even for kicks?" Terry asked.

"So you had no idea her father was an MP?" Sarcasm dripped off Dom's tongue.

Daniel frowned. "Military police? What's that got to do with anything?"

"Member of parliament, you moron. In England." The sharpness was gone from Dom's voice and he looked as though he was trying not to laugh.

"Oh, sorry. No, had no idea. American politics are confusing enough. I don't have the stamina to take on the British."

"How do we know you're not conning us now?" Terry demanded.

Daniel opened his mouth, but Dom cut him off. "Matches the info I got from New York. Even the bit about the money and the agent."

"And dear old Dad?" Colin avoided looking at Lana.

With a knowing smirk, Dom shook his head. "Doesn't seem to be ringing any bells with him, and I would be able to tell. I interview a lot of people. I can smell a lie like a fart."

Daniel hoped Lana could believe him. "To answer your question, you don't know if I'm telling the truth. I have no credibility. There's not a thing I can say to convince you."

Dom's expression softened and his lips twitched. "That was the right answer."

"Do you still work?" The bitter disgust had left Lana's voice.

"I couldn't paint for a long time. Not until I saw you." Daniel looked directly at Lana, and this time she met his gaze. "I've started again, and I think I'm painting better than before."

He went to the covered easel and pulled off the drape. The painting he revealed was an abstract, but in contrast to the dark, stabby paintings leaning against the wall, this one was serene, giving an impression of water flowing in a river, all shades of blue, aqua, and green.

"It's beautiful." Lana left the window for the first time since she'd retreated there.

"That's how you make me feel."

Lana stood so close Daniel could smell her. Her lips curved into a smile as she examined the painting.

Maybe there was still some hope. Daniel turned to face the dwarfs. "Well? I know you have no reason to trust me, but I don't want her money or—"

"Good luck getting any money from *her*!" Colin snickered. "She spends everything on her clothes."

Lana ignored him and continued to drink in the painting.

"Money isn't what I'm after," Daniel repeated to Lana. "I just want you."

The three dwarfs looked at one another. "Dom, you're the grand, high assessor of truth. What do you think?" Terry asked.

Dom's sigh was audible to all. His eyes pleading, he looked at Lana like a puppy dog begging for a bone. "We've done what we can to dig up the dirt on Daniel. But I have to admit I sort of believe that he's on the up—"

Terry cut in. "And that's saying something, coming from Dom. Suspicious is his middle name."

Daniel ignored the dwarfs and spoke as if only Lana could hear him. "You have no reason in the world to believe in me, I know—but I've changed. I'm not the same man I was then."

129

"It's up to you, Lana. After all is said and done, it's your decision." Dom shifted from one foot to the other.

LANA LOOKED around at each of her friends, studying their faces. Anxiety, resignation, and even a bit of dawning happiness. For her.

Her anger at Dom drained away when she saw how he was shaking. However overbearing he could be, she knew he cared about her. Perhaps more than anyone else in the world.

"That *was* the right answer, Dom. It is up to me." Purposely, Lana repeated Dom's words. She looked directly at him and smiled. "I appreciate everything you all have done for me."

Relief washed over his face. "Are we still friends?"

Lana went to hug him. "Always, Happy. No matter what." She released him and then hugged Colin and Terry before turning back to Dom. "But don't think your name gives you the right to order me around."

"Happy? What's that got to do with the price of tea in China?" Dom's grin was sly but apologetic.

"Shut up, Dom." Lana laughed. "You dwarfs screw off." She jerked her thumb at the door.

"You want us to hang around outside for a while?" Colin asked.

"If he gets fresh, I'll kick him in the nuts," Lana said.

"Where's the element of surprise if you warn him beforehand what you're going to do?" Terry wondered aloud.

"Listen, Hunter, now that you've revealed your sinful past, I think it's only fair you should know the worst about Lana." Colin paused a couple of beats to heighten the anticipation. "She can't cook to save her life."

Terry started to laugh, but Dom's smile was faint.

Lana shook her head and sighed. "Thank you for sharing that, Bashful. Listen, boys, I appreciate you arranging this intervention, but I think we can take it from here."

Lana put her arms around Dom again to reassure him that she really had forgiven him. "Thanks, Dom. I know you're the brains of this ungodly operation."

"Stay safe, Lana." Dom squeezed Lana tight before letting go. "Love you."

"Love you too."

LANA WATCHED the three men go down the stairs. She listened for the sound of the latch when the flat door shut behind them.

"Think they have their ears pressed to the door?" Daniel asked.

"Probably," Lana said. "I shouldn't complain. They're why I'm still alive."

"So where do we go from here?" Daniel asked.

"How about the Eiffel Tower?" Lana said. "If you haven't been to the top yet—"

"I like the way you think!" Daniel chuckled, even though he was clearly still rattled. "The biggest phallic symbol in Paris. It's very appropriate considering I pack a mean p—"

"No dick jokes," Lana begged.

"I was going to say picnic lunch," Daniel said.

"In drizzling rain? You have hopes." Lana buttoned her coat and led the way down the stairs, aware of Daniel hurrying after her.

After Daniel had pulled on a trench coat, he opened the door to the flat without attempting to touch Lana.

They emerged onto the street without a dwarf sighting, but Lana suspected her friends were still hanging about nearby.

Daniel took Lana's umbrella and held it up over her as they walked, although he kept his distance. Finally he broke the silence. "Confession is said to be good for the soul."

"Maybe I should try it sometime. After a meeting with my boss, just drop the bombshell and stand back to watch the splash."

"I don't know about your boss, but after you honored me by telling me about yourself, I was planning to come clean with you. I knew I had to if I was going to get what I wanted."

"And what do you want?" Lana fought back a sudden swell of emotion. If he answered wrong, she would have to find the strength to walk away. This might be her last chance to find a man who wanted her as she was.

"I wasn't looking for a pretty boy in a dress. I was looking for you. It doesn't matter what you wear. If I hadn't found you, I would have just had to go on looking. And I think you were looking for me."

"Kismet?" Laughter bubbled up inside her, but she managed to keep it inside. He got it after all. "Maybe I was. It's pretty to think so."

"I know what I did in the past was horrible. Looking back now, I can't even understand how I could do it, but that was another life ago."

"I had a past life too."

"Then maybe you'll understand. I never knew what love was until I found you. I never felt even a twinge before, but that's how I felt when I saw you. Like we fit together perfectly." Daniel stopped walking, and Lana turned under the umbrella to face him. "There are dark places in my soul that only you can illuminate."

"Thank God you didn't say that in front of the dwarfs."

"Don't laugh at me," Daniel begged.

"I wasn't really. I only meant this is something I want to keep for only us."

Daniel's smile was still uncertain. "The more I learn about you, the deeper I fall. I know someday I'll hurt you through stupidity or by accident, but never on purpose. I hope you can believe that."

"I do now. I hated Dom for forcing the issue, but perhaps it was for the best."

"I kept putting it off. It's hard to bare the ugly man I became. When I was a kid, I never thought I could—" Daniel broke off and shuddered.

"That's what life does to us. We all start out bright and shiny and new and full of hope, and then…." Lana pulled down her scarf to reveal the raised scars on her throat.

Daniel clenched his jaw so tight Lana heard the snick of his teeth coming together. "So that's why you always wear a—" His expression morphed quickly from rage to grief to understanding. His hand shook as he traced over the red lines on Lana's throat. "If they intended to kill you, they should have cut across, not vertically. They must not have studied anatomy."

Lana trembled at the delicate touch on the ugly marks. "I didn't ask to see his credentials. He didn't seem in practice, but that wasn't much comfort at the time."

"Why did he do it? Was it a boyfriend?"

"I told you I never dated."

"Then why?"

"Some people are offended by what I am. But he didn't kill me, and he didn't win. I'm still here."

Daniel said, "So we're both scarred."

"But perhaps we both can overcome them."

"You already have," Daniel said. "Maybe that's what drew me to you. That incandescence in your eyes."

"That sounds so noble. And here I thought it was my ass." Lana raised a tragic hand to her brow.

"Don't worry, I love your ass too." Daniel snickered and the pain in his eyes cleared.

"Was it love at first sight?"

"Close enough. I admired your appearance when I first saw you. Then we talked and I thought you were the most exquisite creature I'd ever seen, inside and out, but I really fell head over heels when you educated me about the socks."

Lana laughed. "I suppose my job is paying off after all."

"Tell me how you ended up in Paris."

"That was a long road. When I was fifteen, my parents caught me trying on my sister's clothes. They didn't approve of my 'lifestyle choices.' They threw me out or I ran away, or maybe both. It doesn't really matter. It was a long time ago."

"Right when they discovered you?"

"No, first they brought me to shrinks who told them that I couldn't be cured because I wasn't sick. They didn't want to hear that, so they—invited me to leave. I started living on the streets."

"That's... young. I don't have kids, but I can't imagine just... tossing one out."

Lana shrugged. "They had others at home. An heir and a spare. And a *genuine* daughter."

"How did you survive?"

"The dwarfs helped me. They'd give me money when they could, and Dom brought me food." Lana shivered at the memory of that terrifying time. "But they were kids too. What could they do?"

"Next time I see them I'm going to shake their hands." Daniel stared at her bared throat. "Will you tell me how this happened?"

Lana realized she was folding the end of her scarf into progressively smaller triangles and stopped herself. She covered her throat again and knotted the scarf to keep it in place. "Maybe another time."

Daniel reached up to rub his eyes vigorously. "But you lived."

"If Dom hadn't found me, I might not have. I owe him my life."

"Okay, now I want to kiss him."

"He might enjoy that. He's gay too." Lana laughed wickedly at the look of dismay on Daniel's face.

"He's so not my type," Daniel said in a hurry.

"I'm glad to hear that, because I'm not sharing."

Daniel grinned at that. "Neither am I. What happened when Dom found you?"

Lana skipped over the details. She wasn't ready to delve into this right now. She wasn't sure she ever would be. "Oh, he called the police. They informed my parents. After I got out of hospital, I was sent directly to private school that was a cross between an asylum and a prison. It was better than the streets. While I was there, I learned how to fight and fuck."

"All you need for a career in fashion." Daniel's hand was tight around hers, but he matched Lana's light tone. "It's a competitive field."

"But once I turned eighteen, I was on my own again."

"So no one cared about you?"

"No one except for the Three Musketeers. All for one and one for all." Lana chuckled. "When the school booted me, they were outside waiting for me. Dom gave me a dress, Colin had the shoes, and Terry brought makeup."

"Their hearts are in the right place, at least." Daniel laughed. "I hope it was a good outfit."

"Hideous! A dowdy, mumsy little floral. Dom doesn't have an artistic bone in his body." Lana shook her head at the memory. "And don't get me started on the granny slides, but I didn't care. I changed into those girl clothes and never looked back."

"Where did you go?"

"Dom took me home with him. He was at university and sharing a cheap flat with another boy. It was all he had to offer, but he helped me get a job."

"I'm amazed that you were able to make it through that."

"There are times I am too, but I was determined not to be held hostage to that bastard forever." She pointed up at the Eiffel Tower, the top vanishing into gray mist. "Look. We're in Paris. Sometimes I have to pinch myself because I can hardly believe it."

Daniel stared at Lana rather than the building. "And you've kept that whole thing secret all this time? It must have been hard."

"The dwarfs know." Lana ducked out from under the umbrella. She raised her face to feel the rain on it and closed her eyes, knowing Daniel would be there to catch her. "I feel as light as if I'm floating on top of water."

She opened her eyes to find him smiling at her.

"As if the weight has been lifted." He said it not as a question but like a man who knew. "Shall we go home before you get soaked?"

"Only if you beg," Lana teased.

"I'm begging." Daniel held up the umbrella for her to come under. When she did, he put an arm around her. "Your face is wet."

"Like the heavens are washing me clean."

"I want to make love to you, Lana."

Lana laughed. "I wanted that the first time we met. On the table, under the table, to hell with innocent bystanders."

Daniel laughed but then suddenly snatched Lana close and kissed her.

Lana's heart started to race, and she was instantly hard.

When the need for air became pressing, she pushed at Daniel reluctantly, and he ended the kiss but continued to hold Lana close.

"Tu m'enivres. You intoxicate me." Lana shuddered with desire when Daniel breathed the words into her ear. "Let's go home."

Lana looked around. Not one innocent bystander seemed to care about them or even take notice. She smiled and slid her arm around Daniel's waist, and they walked home pressed tightly together.

CHAPTER 9

LANA'S UMBRELLA was lying on the floor in a puddle where they'd abandoned it, along with Daniel's overcoat and her coat, scarf, and soaked sneakers. They got back just in time. Outside came the faint rumble of thunder, and the smell of rain drifted in a window.

Daniel put on some music and held out his arms invitingly.

"What sort of music is this?"

"Old pop standards. Julie London. This one is for the two of us." Daniel started to sing along to "I Bruise Easily."

Lana came willingly into his arms, and Daniel closed his eyes, pressing his cheek against hers. Not really dancing, they stood pressed together and swayed in time to the meaningful lyrics delivered in a smoky purr.

She was in his arms at last, the one person he'd ever had to work that hard to seduce. Daniel was content to take it slow. He could get sex anywhere, but love made everything so different. He didn't want to leave a mark on Lana, except on her heart. Holding her with infinite care, he inhaled her warmth and scent. If she changed her mind, he would release her instantly, even though it would kill him. With his palm flat on the small of her back, he stroked his thumb lightly over her sweater and felt her lean into his touch. In response, she pulled Daniel hard against her.

As perfectly as if they'd rehearsed it, they tilted their heads to fit their mouths together. He leaned in closer and nibbled delicately on her lower lip. She made no sound but parted her lips slightly in invitation, and he slid his tongue between them for his first taste of her.

Blood surged in his veins as he worked his hand under Lana's sweater and slowly untucked her blouse. Daniel inched his hand beneath

137

the fabric to explore the smooth skin of Lana's back. She broke the kiss and arched against Daniel with a tiny gasp of hunger.

Taking his time, Daniel spread his hand wide across her lower back, deliberately keeping his hand still so she could call a halt at any time. Just a few inches of bare skin and Daniel throbbed with desire.

Sliding his fingertips up the curve of Lana's spine, Daniel stopped at the band of her bra. His lips against the soft skin of her throat, he muttered, "Still got that pepper spray handy?"

He felt the tremor of Lana's chuckle. Her voice was husky and low, and the mere sound had him hard as rock.

"I'm taking a leap of faith this time."

"I don't want to rush you."

"I can always say no."

"I want you to feel safe."

"I do." She smiled at him.

Suddenly Daniel was completely disoriented, flying through the air to land flat on his back with a thud. When he caught his breath, he shook his head to clear it and grinned up at Lana. "Okay, I understand why you feel safe. Good thing the rug is so thick."

Lana grinned back. "I took that into account when I selected a landing pad."

Daniel raised himself up onto his elbows. "Self-defense course?"

"Small-circle jujitsu. Dom has a black belt and he dragged me along, you know, after…." Lana pressed her lips tightly together.

"Remind me to thank him for that." Quick as lightning, Daniel struck, sweeping Lana's feet out from under her and yanking her down into his arms. "Gotcha."

She laughed up at him. "Only because I wanted you to."

Daniel loosened his grip to a caress. "I want to make love to you."

Doubt clouded Lana's eyes.

"It'll be all right," Daniel reassured her. "I know what I'm doing."

"You've done this before… with a boy?" Her body went rigid beneath him as she waited for his answer.

"I've had boys and I've had girls, but I've never made love to anyone before the way I'm going to with you."

Daniel leaned in until a mere whisper of space separated their lips, and held his breath as he waited for Lana to decide. He touched her face, his heart beating fast. Whatever Lana saw when she looked into his eyes translated through her body. Daniel felt her soften and mold herself against him. She leaned up to press her mouth against his. The kiss that started out soft and lush became more demanding.

They broke apart and he looked at her, flushed and panting for air.

"I want you like I've never wanted anyone before," Daniel whispered. He dropped light kisses all along her jawline. As she raised her chin to give him access, he licked the smooth skin of her Adam's apple.

When Daniel insinuated his thigh between Lana's, a soft sigh drifted by his ear. Lana pressed up against him, the friction glorious even through their clothing, her hardness a delicious surprise pressed against his own aching erection. Even though he needed more, Daniel wished the kiss could go on forever. He wanted to drown in it.

Finally Lana broke away and sat up, panting through swollen lips to regain her breath. She laid both hands flat on Daniel's chest. Hoping he provided whatever reassurance she was looking for, Daniel allowed her to search his eyes and remained quite still other than the breathless rise and fall of his chest. His jeans grew even tighter and in desperation, he reached down to adjust himself.

Her gaze followed the movement of his hand, and then she looked up at him and smiled.

A tremulous smile of mingled fear and courage. He wanted to kiss her again and erase all her doubts. When she stood up, Daniel almost reached for her in a panic, fearing she was leaving him.

But Lana shook her head and pressed him down again.

Lana got to her feet, and standing over him, she pulled the sweater over her head. Her hair fell in wild tangles over her face and shoulders, and her shirt was rucked up, exposing her flat stomach.

Her eyes almost defiant, Lana slowly began to unbutton her shirt. She paused once to stroke the scars on her throat as they were fully revealed. Her finger trembled visibly as she touched the raised skin. She hesitated before pulling the edges of her shirt apart to expose her bra.

Catching his breath at the sight of the flat chest, Daniel licked his lips at the hint of enticing nipples visible through the filmy fabric of her bra. The tension built between them until Daniel felt compelled to break it. "I think the cat is out of the bag now."

Startled, Lana stared at him and then cracked up. "That's so not flattering. The bags are supposed to keep them in."

Relieved he hadn't offended her, Daniel chuckled. "Do you—" Daniel had to clear his throat. "Do you *know* how damn desirable you are?"

The smile faded from Lana's lips and she whispered, "No. Tell me."

"Watching you unbutton that shirt, the first glimpse of skin, that bra...." He clenched his hands to stop himself from reaching for her.

Determination on her face, Lana unfastened her jeans. They were tight enough she had to shimmy them down her hips, taking her socks with them. She stepped out of the crumpled jeans and then stood with her hands on her hips, as if daring him to reject her now.

Daniel couldn't stop staring. He had already seen the marks engraved forever on her throat. The creamy, pale skin on the underside of her arms was crisscrossed with scars, no doubt etched into her flesh when she tried to ward off the attack. A crooked line traversed her ribs like a dim trail scribed into a landscape, faded now like a distant memory but still perceptible. The marks on her skin roused an odd combination of tenderness and desire in Daniel, but then the person who stood before him awaiting judgment was an oddly beautiful fusion of masculine and feminine.

Bravery won out over doubt in her eyes, and she stood waiting, her body sleek, bones delicate and fine, offering her vulnerability as a gift. The silky pouch barely contained the evidence of her arousal. The distinct shape of her balls hung heavy at the bottom. Glistening with wetness, the tip of her erection protruded from of the top of her thong.

He wanted to lick the drop off and savor the taste of her. Spread the fluid over the head before sucking the shaft into his mouth. But first Daniel needed to convince Lana of her own magic, because he was assuredly bewitched.

"You are so incredibly and unbelievably beautiful." He reached up and brushed the backs of his fingers over the bulge, watching her shiver in response. "Where have you been all my life?"

"Hanging around Paris waiting for you to come to your senses."

"Come being the operative word. Hot damn!"

"Then you're not disappointed?" A corner of her mouth quirked up.

"I love your parts, but your parts are not why I'm in love with you. I want you more than ever."

Lana's face was pale now where she'd been flushed before, but a relieved smile crept over her face. "That was the right answer."

"It's okay if you have second thoughts. We don't have to do anything right now." Lies! His cock was about to mount an armed coup, but Daniel needed Lana to be sure. Once he had her, he couldn't bear it if she changed her mind.

"I do want to. I really want to."

"Then what are you still doing up there?" Daniel reached for his new lover and pulled her down against him. "I can't resist you. I think I'm already addicted and I've barely had a taste." He kissed along the sculpted line of Lana's jaw, down her throat, lingering over the raised scars to delicately lick away the echoes of pain, before continuing down the smooth chest until he found one of Lana's nipples, capturing it with his lips through the bra. He scraped his stubble gently over the nub before sucking it into his mouth.

Closing her eyes, Lana arched up to chase Daniel's mouth. "Touch me, it's been so long…." She grabbed the back of Daniel's head to hold him to her chest.

He came up for air and kissed his way to the other nipple. "For me too."

Daniel groaned at the pressure of his cock against his jeans. The build of heat and arousal was a familiar sensation, but the person he was doing this with made everything seem brand-new. Distracted by the importance of what was happening, he snapped back to attention when he felt Lana's hands move. He opened his eyes to see her reach back as if to release her bra. "No, leave it on. You look pretty in it."

"You like me in this?" Lana looked down at her nipples, prominent and pushing against the lace.

If she needed reassurance, that's what he would give her. Daniel rubbed both thumbs over Lana's nipples and felt her tremble under his caress. "The bra is beautiful, but I like what's in it better."

"You have an underwear fetish?" Lana's voice was low and breathless.

"More of a Lana fetish, in or out of the bra." Daniel reached down to press his hand against his throbbing erection. He chuckled at his own eagerness, although his laugh sounded more desperate than amused. He felt as oversexed as if he was a teenager again. "Let's move this to the bedroom."

Lana patted the floor gently. "Yeah, this rug isn't that thick."

"Thick enough to toss me on, but not soft enough for the princess?"

"And don't you forget it, sunshine." Lana grinned at Daniel.

Daniel rose and extended a hand to her. "I've got supplies in the bedroom."

As soon as he'd pulled Lana to her feet, Daniel caught her in his arms and kissed her again. "Shall we?"

She didn't answer in words but pressed hard against him, her body language screaming, *Yes, please, more.*

Lana responded to his kiss with more confidence this time, quiet except for her panting for air at intervals in the kiss.

"Did they teach you kissing at that school?"

Lana shook her head. The corners of her mouth turned up in a smile. "Had to learn that on my own."

"Naturally talented, then." Starting in the little hollow between her collarbones, Daniel kissed his way to her shoulder while Lana yanked Daniel's shirt from his jeans. Then she circled her arms around him, pulling him closer as she worked her fingers under his waistband.

Daniel closed his eyes and panted as her fingers dug into his buttocks. He thrust forward, grinding against her. "Or maybe we won't make it all the way up the stairs."

Lana's pupils were dilated, her huge eyes almost black with desire. "That rug is looking better and better." Her voice was as hoarse as his.

Daniel picked her up and knelt to set her down on the rug with tender care. "Should have lit a fire."

"I think you already did." Lana reached up to pull Daniel down.

On his knees, he bent to kiss her again, still struggling with the buttons of his shirt. Finally he gave up and ripped it open, barely registering the tiny click of escaping buttons as they bounced off the rug onto the hardwood floor.

When he let himself down on top of her, they both let out a gasp. At the first moment of contact when skin touched hot skin, he jerked away as if stung by a static shock. But only for a moment before he was back for more. He pulled her closer for a hard kiss and the energy that sparked between them turned into lightning, crackling with heat and desire.

Lana hooked a leg around the back of Daniel's thigh to keep him pressed against her, flexing her hips against his.

Daniel almost laughed into the kiss when he felt Lana's palm pressed hard against the front of his jeans, but he broke away and sat up to take his shirt off.

Lana ran her hands over his chest and stomach with a smile he hadn't seen from her before. His muscles twitched out of control under her touch.

"I have to—have to—" His brain wasn't able to come up with the words. Daniel rolled off her and stood up to rip off his jeans and shorts. His cock snapped up and hit his stomach alertly when released from its prison. He sighed in relief.

"Holy Eiffel Tower! You weren't kidding!" Lana slid her tongue over her lower lip when she saw him for the first time.

Daniel laughed. He was shaky with desire, sweating in the heated air, even though there was no fire in the fireplace and the room was cool.

She reached for him.

Her gasp was loud in his ear when his weight pinned her. He rolled off to the side, wanting their first time to be slow and gentle for her to remember. They moved slowly together, exploring each other's skin, tangling bare legs freed from the clothing that kept them apart.

His hands trembled with need, but he caressed her carefully. Slowly. Daniel groaned in frustration when Lana, not sharing his restraint, wrapped her fingers around his shaft and pumped it. "Going to last about ten seconds if you keep doing that."

"Me too."

In one last gasp of sentience, Daniel lifted his head and grinned. "This time. Next time, watch out—ahh, fuck!" He rolled on top of her, covering her body with his. His mind dissolved as Lana ground against him, pressing their hard cocks together. The thin silk of her thong provided an extra frisson of pleasure.

She gripped his hair, holding his head in place as their tongues danced frantically between their open mouths, mirroring the convulsive thrust of their hips.

As they rocked together in abandon, Daniel knew he was done for. He wrenched his mouth free and let out a groan as he exploded. He felt her cock pulse against his through the thong, and that pushed him over the edge. He came hard, crying out as he did. A moment later he heard the release of her breath as she came and their semen mingled between their bodies.

After a moment frozen in place like a silent statue, Daniel collapsed on the rug, breathing hard. He needed to feel Lana against him. He rolled onto his side and pulled her closer. She slung a leg over his and lay there panting with her eyes closed.

"As controlled as a couple of teenagers," Daniel muttered.

A faint murmur was the only answer, but he couldn't make out the words.

Finally Daniel reached up and brushed the hair off Lana's face. Now that his breathing had returned to near normal, he could hear the gentle sound of rain on the windows. "That was just a warm-up."

Lana started in on another fit of the giggles. "Oh, I'm warm, believe me."

"No, you're insanely and unimaginably hot."

She yawned widely between giggles. "And somewhat sleepy. Can we risk a short nap?"

Daniel snickered. "Recharge the batteries?"

"Sounds like a plan."

"I'll be right back." Reluctantly, but as a good host does, Daniel climbed the stairs on weak legs to find a washcloth. He cleaned himself off and rinsed it out. Then he took the washcloth downstairs to find that Lana had stripped off her underwear. She was sitting up and blinking sleepily.

Too tired to take time to fully appreciate her, Daniel offered the washcloth. She took it and wiped her stomach before flopping down onto her back.

Daniel retrieved the cloth and dropped it onto the stone hearth. Then he reached for a throw on the back of the couch and put it over her.

Lana lifted the blanket. "Get back here."

Daniel snuggled up against her, pulling her close. So drained he was no longer able to think or function, Daniel stopped fighting it and succumbed to the need to sleep.

THE AIR was cool on her skin where she wasn't pressed against something warm and solid. Lana wondered where she was, but even more, whose naked body was pressed against her. Then her eyes popped open and memory came back in a heady rush. She was on her side, and behind her, Daniel was curled around her, one arm reaching around to cross her chest. She had a firm grip on his hand, holding it in place. She moved against him, hungry for the luxury of bare skin touching skin.

She laughed in delight to herself, but at the quiet sound, Daniel's breathing hitched and his body jerked. "Forget where you were?"

Daniel chuckled. "I've never slept on this rug before, not that I ever had such a good reason, but you were right. It's not thick enough." He moved her hair to nuzzle the back of her neck. "And we have some unfinished business."

Lana's stomach growled. "I think I need to eat first. I didn't have time for breakfast before Dom dragged me over here."

Daniel's arm moved as he checked his watch. "Damn, it's two o'clock. You must be starving. This is a horrible dilemma, sex or food, but I guess I'd better feed you if I want a willing participant."

"Oh, I'm willing, I just might not remain conscious if I don't eat something." Lana sat up and ran her fingers through her hair, lifting it back over her shoulders. "Shall we dine al fresco?"

"If by that you mean naked, wonderful idea." Daniel pushed himself up to his feet and stretched.

She watched as he extended his arms over his head and yawned, his cock hanging heavy and halfway hard already. His broad shoulders tapered to a narrow waist and hips, his chest was muscular, and his arms were defined with muscle. "You're beautiful too."

Daniel offered his hand. "Glad you like what you see."

Lana allowed him to bring her to her feet. Then he pulled her against him and wrapped his arms around her. "Mmm, skin."

"Mmm, food," she reminded him, although he felt better than any breakfast could taste.

He led her into the kitchen and opened the refrigerator. "Let's see, milk, coffee beans, some carrots neatly arranged in the crisper, and a large selection of condiments. Unless you can make do with a carrot, pickles, and hot sauce on the side, there's not much choice. I usually get takeaway."

She peered over his shoulder to view the empty interior. "I can't complain. This looks exactly like my refrigerator."

"Another thing we have in common. Well, there's always cereal." He closed the fridge and went to a cupboard to get two bowls. Then he crossed the room and opened a door that turned out to be a pantry. Triumphantly, Daniel displayed a box of American cereal. "At least I have milk."

They ate standing up at the counter, eyeing each other's naked body the whole time. Within minutes, they'd polished off their breakfast. Daniel took her bowl and put it into the sink with his.

The first time had started off slow and careful. Daniel had taken care to avoid even the suggestion of coercion.

But now as they stood facing each other in the kitchen, Lana didn't want careful. She wanted to be swept away by a storm of passion, and by the look in his eye, Daniel did too. Lana had never expected to find someone willing to accept her, much less delight in her, but here he was at last, and standing within easy reach. They slammed together like a wave crashing over a rocky shore.

Lana's breath huffed out when her back hit the cool plaster wall. Daniel's weight held her in place as she hauled him closer. His knee nudged insistently, and she spread her legs to make room for it, gasping as their groins came together. Any lingering doubt about how just much he wanted her vanished. Could anyone fake that?

Daniel latched onto her neck, sucking and licking in a flurry of kisses while he slid his hands down her flanks. Heat flared through her body, and she wasn't positive she could have stayed on her feet without Daniel's weight holding her up.

His hands were on her buttocks, squeezing each cheek. Lana tilted her head back as Daniel grazed her neck lightly with his teeth, erasing each nip with a swipe of his tongue. Leaning her head against the wall, Lana closed her eyes and strained to pull Daniel in tighter, lifting one leg to wrap it around his waist. Their cocks bumped together, a tease of what was hopefully to come.

Daniel whispered into her ear, his breath coming in rhythmic gasps. "You got the short tour earlier. Want me to show you the bedroom?"

"I can think of many things I'd like you to show me." She still enjoyed the soft pressure of his lips and the taste of him, but the unyielding hardness of the wall against her shoulder blades ruined the setting. "This wall is even less comfortable than the rug."

"Sorry, sorry. Just got a little carried away." He peeled her off the wall and started backing out of the kitchen toward the stairs, staring into her eyes. He chuckled when he stumbled into a chair. "Clearly not the most efficient way to change locations."

She smiled up at him. "And what would be?"

Lana let out a gasp when Daniel crouched and grabbed an arm and a leg, yanking her down over his shoulder. Then he lifted her off her feet and grunted. "You're heavier than you look."

"Because I'm all muscle. Don't break your back." Even hanging upside down, Lana had to laugh when he sprinted for the stairs. She braced herself against his back. "Show-off."

In her wildest fantasy, she'd never pictured this, but apparently Daniel could make her like it, even though his shoulder was digging into her solar plexus.

When they arrived in the bedroom, Daniel gently set Lana on her feet in front of the bed.

"Nice room." Without a single glance around, she fell back onto the mattress and pulled Daniel down with her. Her hand cupping the back of his neck, Lana hauled him closer for a kiss. With her fingertips, she traced down Daniel's spine from the nape of his neck to the tailbone and back up to the top again.

Then she gasped and arched into his touch when he pinched a nipple.

"Hot spot?" Daniel touched his forehead to hers.

She closed her eyes and shivered as he did it again, tugging harder this time. "You could... say that."

"I'd better check if there are any others."

His lips traced a lazy path down her body. Then a sudden swipe of wet tongue over the head of her cock had Lana writhing and grabbing the sheets as if they alone could keep her from flying away. She bit her lips to keep a moan inside.

Then Daniel ran his hands up and down the sensitive skin of her inner thighs and she spread her legs for more. As she thrust up into empty air, Daniel nuzzled under her cock and sucked in one of her balls, tonguing it thoroughly before moving to the other.

She made a thin sound of protest when he stopped.

"Open your eyes, babe."

"I can't," she whispered, suddenly engulfed by emotion.

Now Daniel's mouth was on her jaw, her neck, the curve of her shoulder, leaving hot kisses on her skin. "Why not?" His teeth scraped her skin lightly and with infinite care. His tongue followed, painting a hot trail that cooled almost immediately, leaving her to shiver.

"I don't know." Lana held him off with a trembling hand and took several deep breaths. Finally she managed to open her eyes.

"It's all right." Daniel was looking at her with concern. "We can take a time-out."

She twined her fingers with his. "I'm sorry, it's just a bit overwhelming all of a sudden."

"We don't have to take this too fast." His appearance said otherwise. Daniel was breathing hard, and a sheen of sweat shone on his chest. "Why don't we do this instead?"

149

He rolled onto his back, his cock standing up hard and proud, and folded his hands behind his head. "Have your way with me." His eyes twinkled as he spoke, and Lana couldn't help laughing.

The fact that he was trying to make this as easy as possible gave her the push she needed. Lana sat up and swung her leg over his, straddling his thighs. She wiggled closer to line up their cocks. His balls felt full and firm under hers, like tiny eager pillows bearing her aloft. She circled her hips a bit to rub them together. Although apparently trying to remain still, Daniel failed, grabbing for the sheets. His hips started to flex, compounding the aching heat in her balls.

He stared up at her, but when she reached for his cock, he lifted his head to watch.

Lana swiped her thumb over the head and then stroked down the length of Daniel's hard shaft.

He bucked his hips up, almost unseating her. "Holy fuck, Lana."

His cock solid and thick in her hand, Lana slid her thumb and forefinger down his length, her lower lip caught between her teeth.

Without a word, Daniel stretched and reached behind him, yanking open a drawer in the nightstand. She heard the click of the flip-top when he opened the bottle and then offered it to her.

Lana slicked up her hands, and Daniel let out a little yelp when she started at the base with a few light strokes. He grabbed for the sheets when she lined up their cocks, as if he needed an anchor.

If she moved, she would come all over him right now. The sensitive undersides of their cocks rubbed together in the most tantalizing way. Maybe it was the quivering of his muscles beneath her, or possibly it was her own body shaking like an aspen leaf in the wind. Lana tried to remain still. Daniel held his breath but waited for her to make the first move.

After Lana fought down the urge to rut mindlessly against him, she started a slow rhythm with both hands clasped around their cocks. Instantly her hips started to thrust as if no longer under her control, grinding against Daniel in need of more friction, more stimulation.

Daniel groaned and reached for Lana's hands, letting his ride up and down resting loosely on hers.

Watching Daniel tremble, hearing him moan with every breath, almost gave her greater pleasure than the sensations of their cocks sliding together as she built to a crescendo.

She sped up the action of her hand and Daniel surged up under her. She shifted her weight to hold him down, and then he was coming, spurting come over her hand and shouting out his pleasure without inhibition. "I'm going to...."

Watching him come was more than she could withstand. Lana bit back a moan as her orgasm shook her like an earthquake, sweeping away all conscious thought. Then she collapsed forward on Daniel, tiny aftershocks rolling through her body.

The comforting touch of his hands tracing circles on her back brought Lana back.

"Oh fuck." Daniel's words came out on a groan. "That was so hot on so many levels, I can't even...."

He held on to her and rolled to the side, taking her with him so they were lying face to face. "How do you manage to keep so quiet? I was screaming so loud I thought the neighbors would call the cops."

"No sign of them yet," Lana mumbled into his shoulder. She grinned when Daniel laughed.

"Just lucky I guess. Are you going to answer my question, or would you prefer not to talk about it?"

"You're giving me a choice?" Lana opened her eyes to look at him.

He raised his brows in surprise. "Of course. Why would I ever force the issue? And even more to the point, how?"

"I suppose I'm used to the dwarfs. They tend to put the pressure on."

"Yeah, I've noticed they are just a bit pushy. Particularly when they put me under house arrest today." An off note in Daniel's voice told Lana he had not enjoyed that part of the program.

"So does this mean it's time to exchange our life stories?"

151

"I admit I'd love to hear yours, but not under duress. If and when you choose to tell me, I'll be ready and waiting." Daniel groaned and sat up. "Back in a minute." He got himself upright in stages and padded across the room to the bathroom and closed the door.

She heard a flush and then water running in the sink.

He opened the door and came out with a washcloth in his hand, but she got up herself, combing her hair out of her face with her fingers. "I have to pee too."

From the doorway, he tossed the washcloth into the sink. "Be my guest."

When Lana came out, he had drawn the curtains, turned on a lamp by the bed, and was propped up on pillows against the headboard. The duvet had been turned down, and he'd drawn the sheet up to his waist. When she entered the room, Daniel opened his eyes and patted the mattress beside him. "C'mon over."

Daniel lifted the sheet and Lana slid under it. He put his arm around her and she leaned into him. He rubbed his cheek on the top of her head. "Don't know about you, but I'm gonna be asleep in under a minute."

She closed her eyes. Now that the storm that raged between them was over, the tranquil sound of the rain against the windows pulled her under the waves. "Race you."

Lana heard him mumble something about next time, but she never found out who won.

WARM LIPS on her forehead woke Lana. She sat up and pushed her hair out of her face, looking around in confusion before she realized where she was.

Daniel was dressed, and droplets of rain glistened on his hair as he sat down on the mattress next to her. "I can offer you dinner in bed or you can come downstairs and dine in style."

Did he go out for takeaway? Through the rain, for her. "Food," Lana said thoughtfully. "Sounds like a good plan."

He nodded. "I don't want you to starve to death. So which will it be?"

"We wouldn't want to mess up the bed, would we?"

"We would and we will," Daniel said, "but not with food, unless it involves me licking it off your naked body or vice versa."

She laughed and made a face. "Too messy. Besides, then we'd have to change the sheets or wake up smelling like whatever it is you fetched."

"What makes you think I didn't prepare a feast for you with my own two hands?" Daniel tried to pout and failed because he was grinning.

"Out of carrots and pickles? It was a pretty safe assumption." Lana looked around, searching vaguely for something to wear. "You wouldn't happen to know where my clothes are, would you?"

"They happen to be in the washer right now. But it wouldn't bother me at all if you chose to dine naked. You're very decorative and you spruce the place up. The management has no dress code." Daniel waggled his eyebrows at her.

"Only if you join me." Lana wrapped her arms around herself and shivered.

"You're cold." He stroked her arm. "You've got goose bumps. I'll get you something to put on." Daniel went to the wardrobe and pulled out a silk dressing gown embroidered with peacocks. "I've only worn it a few times. It's practically new."

Lana buried her nose in the silk and sighed. "Mmmm, smells like you." Lana stood up and tied the belt. "I'll be down as soon as I wash my face."

"I'll put the food out." Daniel bent to kiss her and left the room walking backward, staring as if he couldn't believe she was really there.

DANIEL HURRIED downstairs to unpack the bags. Considering the solitary life he'd led since arriving in Paris, he had no dining table or chairs. The single stool in the kitchen worked just fine for one man.

But now he wanted Lana to relax and eating standing up over the sink didn't exactly strike a hospitable note.

He'd taken a chance on Chinese, hoping Lana would like it. The scent of the spicy food made his stomach growl. He set out the containers on the coffee table before hurrying to the kitchen for plates.

On Daniel's return, inspiration struck, and he started a fire to offset the chill in the air. He remembered the window he'd left open and closed it. Listening to the rain outside while sitting by a fire was cozy, even romantic. He was patiently fanning the flames when he caught sight of her coming down the stairs in the brilliant robe much too big for her slender figure. Lana smiled when their eyes met.

"I could eat a horse," she said.

This unromantic pronouncement made Daniel laugh. "I'm glad I got a lot, then. I didn't know what you'd like, so I ordered a variety. I hope you like Chinese."

"I love it."

Another score for him. The fire finally going, he dusted off his hands. Instead of sitting on the couch, Lana sank to the rug by the low table and crossed her legs. Catching her quick sidelong glance at the portrait on the wall, Daniel sat on the floor opposite her so he could see both the painting and the original who inspired it.

They ate in silence until, hunger at least partially appeased, they came up for air.

"This is all so good. Thank you." Lana stole another glance at the painting as if embarrassed at getting caught looking at herself.

Purposely, Daniel turned to face the unfinished portrait. "It doesn't do you justice."

"You see something in me I'm not sure is really there."

"Originally I only wanted to paint you. Of course you're gorgeous, but there was something in your eyes." Daniel kept his gaze on the painting. "When I saw you on the street, I ran after you, just to ask if you'd sit for me. Had the devil of a time catching up to you too."

"I saw you on my street one evening."

He gave a slight nod and bowed his head in remorse. "I was so caught up in finding you, it never occurred to me that I was essentially stalking you until Dom followed me that night. When I realized what I was doing, I decided to come back here and try to paint you from memory."

"It's very good, as a painting I mean."

He grinned thinking about that memorable day. "I threw a brush across the studio in frustration, but I wasn't so far gone as to toss it out the window. It's a good brush. I would have missed it."

Lana laughed. "That would have surprised someone if it fell on them."

"A good portrait takes time to get to know your model. As a painter, I have to decide how my subject wants to see themselves and find a way to flatter and yet still tell the truth. Particularly when you need the money and you have to please a rich client. Ever hear the saying you get the face you deserve by the time you're forty?"

Lana nodded.

"Thoughts and emotions have a way of carving their impression on bone and flesh, and if you're any good, you learn to see through the shield to the essence of people."

"Sounds like a good skill for a painter."

Daniel winced at the thought of some of his past models. "Depends on who you're painting. For me, it was mostly women. A few were genuine, but for the most part, I didn't like what I saw no matter how beautiful the face, which is awkward when you're depending on their generosity. After I'd made a name for myself as a portrait artist, I became fashionable. Everyone had a specific request, like make my nose look better or help me lose ten pounds. I painted to please them."

He pointed at her portrait. "On the other hand, I *loved* every frustrating minute I spent trying to capture you because I painted that to please me. Now that the model is here in front of me, I can see the line of the bottom lip isn't quite perfect. And maybe the angle of the jaw. But your eyes are right, the courage and light glowing out of them is absolutely right. After I painted it, I would sit here and stare at you and burn with longing for what I saw in your eyes."

"And what do you see?" Lana whispered.

"Ironic, considering how you choose to present yourself from the world, but I see you, unmasked. You present the truth of yourself to everyone who has the eyes to see. Whereas I, the clean-cut, all-American blackmailer…." His voice rasped, and he cleared it. "I'm the one who's wearing the mask. Or I used to until wanting you forced me out from undercover."

She stretched her hand over the table to take one of his. "I'm glad you took the mask off and let me see the real Daniel."

He laughed. "And even that isn't my real name."

"What is it?"

"Mervin. Mervin Everhard."

They both burst out laughing.

"I think I'll stick with Daniel, if you don't mind," Lana said.

"I would be grateful. And even more so if you never reveal my name to the dwarfs."

"I think I can promise that. Although, with that rather interesting last name…."

"I'll try to live up to it." Daniel stood up and pulled her to her feet. He leered at her. "At least I have good motivation."

"I'll do my best to inspire you."

"I still want to paint you. A proper portrait. I have a feeling it will take a lifetime to do you justice."

"Can we take a time-out first for more important business?"

"I think I just cleared my calendar for you, Lana Renault."

DANIEL LET out a surprised grunt when Lana grabbed the front of his shirt and pushed him against the wall inside his bedroom door. She kissed him hard enough to bruise, and he pulled her closer. Her sudden attack got him hard in seconds. Although slim, Lana was strong enough to hold him still, at least when he was totally weak in the knees. She unbuttoned his shirt to trace her fingers lightly over his chest, still keeping her lips on his.

When she got his jeans open and curled her hand around his erection, Daniel tore his mouth away from hers, gasping for air. His head fell back against the wall with a muffled thud, and he couldn't keep his eyes open. The beat of his pulse thundered in his ears because hot… wet… tongue….

He was so lost.

"WHERE DID you learn to do that?" he asked weakly when he could remember the existence of words. He must have made it to the bed somehow, because he was flat on his back staring up at the ceiling.

She laughed. "Don't you remember? I went away to a very exclusive school."

"Oh right, fighting and fucking." Daniel opened his eyes to find her looking very pleased with herself, her eyes aglow. "Sorry, I didn't mean to get so rough with you there."

"Hey, I took it like a man," Lana said with a smirk.

The shock of her comment made him laugh. "I can see we're going to have lots of fun with double entendres."

"I certainly hope so."

Recovering some strength, Daniel reached for the robe and yanked it down her arms. Then he pulled her naked body against his and kissed her.

"When I first met you, I said, 'There is a woman with unplumbed depths.'"

Lana cracked up. "And you wanted to be the one to plumb them."

"What should we do now?"

Lana squinted to glare at him. "The deal was I do you and then you do me. Pay up, buddy boy."

"I plead that the contract wasn't enforceable. I signed under the duress of an urgent need to come."

"We shook hands," she pointed out, her hips starting to undulate.

"You've got me there. Although this isn't exactly a hardship."

Lana pushed his hand away, suddenly looking nervous. "You want to fuck me?"

"I would, after a brief period of recovery. That is, if you go for that kind of thing."

"I go for that kind of thing."

"We can take it slow. I can think of a lot of other things I'd like to do to you." A slight relaxation of rigid muscles told Daniel she needed reassurance. He might not get to fuck her tonight. He might not ever fuck her. Didn't matter. "Do me a favor. If I ever do anything you don't like, even if it's something you asked me to do, stop me. Right then. Don't worry about breaking the mood."

"It's a deal. But so far…." Her slow, wicked smile told him her confidence was back. "I wouldn't change a thing."

For most of his life, getting laid had been the goal, even when servicing a client. He didn't care if they found paradise in his arms or only a good time for an hour or so. He took pride in his sexual prowess, but this was different. Daniel wanted to make Lana feel cared for and cared about. Her silence shook his confidence. "Neither would I. But I think I'm getting a complex. I can't even get a moan out of you."

"I loved every minute, Daniel." In mute apology, Lana reached up to caress his cheek.

"You're so quiet it's a little unnerving."

"You're used to more applause?"

"Maybe you could help my ego out with a little attaboy every now and then?"

"I'll try, but I haven't worn my cheerleader outfit in ages." Lana giggled. "Remember how that school focused on really important life skills?"

"They had a cheer squad there?"

"Of course not. The staff was such a bunch of old fogies they actually told us we weren't supposed to either fight or fuck, but fucking was *really* against the rules, so we had to be silent about it. I guess… I just haven't let go of that."

Keep quiet or else. "Maybe one day you'll feel safe enough to let go with me."

"I hope that too." Blinking rapidly, Lana turned her head, but he caught the glint of unshed tears. "I've been alone a long time. I'm used to...."

"Keeping secrets?" Secrets that are secrets themselves, maybe even to her.

"I've always had to hide the most basic fact about myself."

"I'm sorry you had to. Unwrapping you is like getting the best present I didn't know I wanted on Christmas morning, but with all the frolic and abandon of New Year's Eve rolled in."

Lana grinned and held up both hands. "Ta da!"

He kissed her shoulder. "Hard to believe that someone wants you as is?"

"Yes. It is." Lana looked up at the ceiling before shooting him a sidelong glance. "I never thought this was possible."

"I'm going to take my time and show you how beautiful...." He kissed her forehead. "How amazing...." Daniel nibbled her collarbone. "How very desirable you are."

Lana shivered but kept her gaze locked with Daniel's.

This time he wanted to explore. With a fingertip, he traced the dark arch of her brow, the curve of her cheekbone, wide lips that turned up at the corners as if on the brink of a smile. And even after all that had happened to her, she was totally unselfconscious, splayed out naked on his bed with everything on display. For him. The light of the single lamp caressed Lana's skin, lighting her up like the moon in a dark sky.

He touched his tongue to her throat where he felt the pulse beat rapidly under his tongue. Breathy little sounds escaped her when he touched his lips to the scars on her throat, wishing he could draw out all the bitterness, fear, and pain with his kisses. The planes and angles of her body were beautiful in Daniel's eyes, all subtle curves and hollows. Tracing the satin skin of Lana's chest, he moved lower, intent on the way her abdominal muscles rippled under his fingers. He loved how she arched up into his touch like a cat when he feathered tiny kisses over her skin. The curve of her hip fit perfectly into his palm.

Lana stretched sensuously as Daniel started over at her feet. He massaged the arch of one slender foot, biting into it gently before he released it.

She giggled and tried to pull away. "Tickles."

Daniel stroked up the back of her leg from her calf to the swelling roundness of her buttock. Cupping his palm over the firm globe, he rubbed a slow erotic circle, making her purr in pleasure. The faint lines of her ribs invited his attention, and Daniel slid his hands over her waist. He moved higher to appreciate the strength of her slender arms and elegantly angular shoulders.

Daniel let his tongue linger over a tender pink nipple to hear the little gasps he was sure Lana didn't realize she was making. The tilt of her hips invited Daniel to roam lower; the sheen of sweat on porcelain skin gleamed like a pearl. The flutter of the sensitive skin in the furrow between her body and thigh under Daniel's lips, the low hum of pleasure as Lana allowed her legs to fall open.

Lana moaned as Daniel parted warm thighs to kneel between them, kissing a path up the tender inner surface, the skin silky and hot under his mouth. Daniel ran his hands over the muscles of her thighs. So delicate and yet strong.

Daniel blew warm air across her balls before running his tongue over them, eliciting a surprised squeak as his stubble scratched her tender skin.

"I've got you," Daniel whispered. "Tell me if you want me to stop."

"Please, God, don't stop...." Her voice broke as she pleaded for more.

The taste and scent of her were intoxicating. The sight of Lana all spread out writhing and moaning in his bed reminded Daniel of his aching cock, hard again already. But, determined to please her rather than himself, he ignored his own need. The bead of fluid gleaming on the tip of her cock tempted him beyond measure, and he bent to slake his thirst.

Lana moaned again and louder this time, her hips starting to set a faint rhythm. When Daniel captured the head of her cock in his mouth, a deep groan arose from her throat, and he echoed it. He pressed his tongue on the engorged vein that ran underneath and then released it to feel it fill again. Daniel licked up and down her shaft, taking the time to explore every beautiful inch.

His mouth full of her, his emotions blazed like fire inside him. Lana jerked her hips when he cupped her balls again. Her fingers tightened in his hair.

Her cock swelled in his mouth, filling him even further. She started to thrust wildly and came with a loud cry, calling out his name. Daniel smiled around her cock and swirled his tongue gently around the head one last time.

When her movement stopped, Daniel reverently allowed her limp cock to slide from between his lips.

After taking a moment to catch his breath, Daniel moved up to drop a gentle kiss on Lana's parted lips. "Thank you," he whispered.

He grinned at her faint giggle. Lana opened her eyes. "Isn't that my line after the ultimate blow job?"

"You gave me something too. Something I needed. I loved hearing you let go." Daniel settled himself at her side, propping himself up on his elbow.

"Attaboy."

He sniggered quietly while she rolled into him, burying her face in his neck. "At last. Now I feel vindicated."

"You didn't do it all by yourself, you know. What time is it?"

"The clock hasn't yet struck midnight, my lady. In fact, it's only nine thirty."

"Good, because before it does, we should do it again."

"Again? We just finished."

"Are you complaining?"

"Have mercy. I need time to refill." Daniel wrapped his arms around her. He wasn't ready for these new feelings of tenderness to die away and leave. He hoped they never would.

"Somehow I'm not sleepy this time."

Daniel shook with laughter. "We've passed out twice already. Maybe all we need is a little recovery time."

"Or a bedtime story."

"You can tell me the story of your life now if you want."

"Oh that."

"Or not, if you don't."

"We'll see," Lana said.

CHAPTER 10

LEANING AGAINST the headboard snuggled into Daniel's arms, her pulse slowing from the mad canter of her orgasm, Lana took in a deep breath. "The dwarfs know part of my story because they were there, but I never told them the whole thing."

Daniel was silent, and his warm hands on her skin were still.

The rain was still coming down outside; she heard it spitting on the window. "No one can know everything about another person."

His arms tightened around her. "Probably not. Just tell whatever you want me to know."

"I was five when I started wearing girls' clothes. Somehow I knew it had to be a secret, and I was very good at sneaking into my sister's room when I wouldn't be caught."

"How did you know it had to be a secret?"

"I don't know." Lana took in a deep breath. "My sister wore jeans on weekends, so why shouldn't I wear a dress? I thought it would be okay if I borrowed one as long as I put it back before she found out. Of course I was eventually caught. When my mother saw me in a dress, she nearly scared me to death, she screamed so loud. She was furious and put me in a corner. When my father got home, they talked to me about the devil and how ashamed I should be."

"And were you?"

"No, never. It felt right—*I* felt right wearing those clothes."

"Stubborn little devil."

Lana grinned. "I wasn't very popular in my family."

"And did you realize you were gay then?"

"Of course not. I wasn't exactly weighing the consequences and possibilities for a lifetime of regret. I didn't even know about sex.

How was I to know it was going to turn out to be such a big fucking deal to people?" Lana gave a bitter laugh. "All right, I admit I should have been able to tell from my parents' reactions, but I was only a small child."

"What do you remember most?"

Lana shivered and smiled. "I remember an aqua polka-dotted dress I loved. Learning to walk in heels so big they wouldn't stay on my feet. And listening. I was always listening for a creak of the stairs, a door opening, footsteps."

"That's terrible and sad."

"It wasn't all bad. When I met the dwarfs in kindergarten, they didn't care what I wore or who I thought I was. I was close to all of them, but mostly to Dom, because he turned out to be gay too. I had his back through his coming out, and he's always had mine. To a fault sometimes. I think he has unfulfilled parental needs."

"Yes, he is a tiny bit protective." They both laughed. "And then what happened?"

"I managed to hide my secret from my parents until I was fifteen." Suddenly the river ran dry, and Lana compressed her lips into a tight line. No one knew what had happened that day except three people, she and her parents. Maybe she would be ready to talk about it someday, but not yet. "You already know about the school."

"Ah yes, the famous school." An undertone of anger rumbled in Daniel's light words.

"I was sent there directly from hospital. I never saw my parents again."

"They didn't even come to the hospital?" Daniel was shocked.

"I remember Dom being there. He told the nurses he was my brother so he could get in."

"That explains why you tolerate him." Daniel's smile took the sting out of that comment.

"My parents sent a lawyer—"

"A lawyer?"

"With a contract. They would pay for my schooling until I was eighteen if I agreed to change my name and go away quietly. Of

164

course I didn't realize what sort of school I was being sent to, but I didn't want to be around them any more than they wanted to see me. It was an escape."

"Your father trusted a lawyer with this?"

"Probably had him killed later," Lana joked. "Politics can be cutthroat. Anyone who knows your secret turns into a Sword of Damocles."

"And that's it? Your expenses paid at a school you don't want to be at and don't let the door hit you on the ass on your way out?"

"I was fifteen. Sounded like a good deal to me."

"I remember being fifteen. You think you can do anything but feel like you're nothing. It's a hard age."

"When I graduated from the school at eighteen, the only thing I wanted was to put on a dress. I'd fought so long to be able to, that seemed like the endgame. Once I could wear what I wanted, I thought I'd be happy forever."

"You kind of glossed over what landed you in the hospital."

Lana licked her dry lips. "I did, didn't I?"

"You don't have to talk about it."

"I hate even thinking about it." Her throat closed up unexpectedly, her mind tumbling back to that time. Lana couldn't remember herself at fifteen—somehow that person was unreachable now—but she remembered the world spinning around her, rough skin on the hands hurting her wrists, hot stinking breath, the flash of light from the knife, like a mirror in the sunlight, and she saw herself, short tufts of hair, head almost bald and red like blood, not lipstick. She dug her fingers hard into Daniel's arm, and his hands on her body were patient when she retreated from the alley of her memory, and she knew without telling that he would wait for her to be ready however long it took. "I can't."

"I get it. I don't like talking about my... mine either." Under the rush of her own breath, Daniel's voice sounded as if it was coming from somewhere far away.

"I suppose we have that in common."

"Peas in a pod."

"Two birds of a feather."

"Two of a kind." Lana breathed in Daniel's sigh as if sharing the same sad exhale could make them even closer.

"It taught me, at least, not to do things that make people want to stab you."

"It taught me to keep myself to myself."

"And are the men of Paris blind? No balls? You're worth the effort. Didn't anyone ask you out?"

Lana appreciated Daniel's attempt to steer them off dangerous ground, although even this subject was still a bit touchy. "Sometimes, but of course I couldn't go."

"How did you say no?"

"You put your finger right on the sore spot, because I never have figured out a good way to break the news. By the way, I'm a dude in a dress and the advantage is we'll go dutch!"

"Yeah, there might be better ways."

"The last time I trusted a man enough to tell him, he said, 'You're lucky I'm not crazy, because the next guy might really fuck you up if you lay something like that on him.'"

"Charming." Daniel frowned. "I hate even thinking about it, but I'll bet you've had worse."

"I found that out the hard way. Rejection isn't fun, but it's also scary, and some guys seem to think it's perfectly all right to take things too far."

"How far?" Daniel's face was grim.

"I've been pushed and slapped around a few times. I stopped trying. I accepted that I would be alone. Why risk it?"

"I can't blame you for turning me down when we met, but those assholes are fucking stupid. They may not want to date you, but they don't have to hurt you if they want to say no."

"I fought so hard to be able to wear what I want that I can't knuckle under to someone else's idea of how I ought to be." Lana smiled at the thought of her lovely clothes. "And besides, I love dressing like a woman. I don't *want* to give it up."

166

"That's one of the things I love about you. That passion." Daniel took a breath. "Are you as scared as I am?"

"Of this? Of love? You bet."

"Me too." The muscles of his arms felt hard and solid, but his hands shook as he held her against his chest. "Should we do it anyway?"

"Yes, I think so." She took a deep breath and rested her forehead against his, knowing what the next question would be.

"You can kick me if I'm being tactless," Daniel started.

Warily, Lana nodded. "Go ahead."

"Is Roland ever going to come out to play?"

He surprised her after all. Lana laughed at herself for jumping to conclusions. "Roland is a part of me. He's always with me, when I play, when I work. I don't hate the male part of myself. Obviously—I was born a boy—but I just like wearing feminine clothing to express a softer side of myself. And they're so much prettier."

"And the pronouns?"

"I prefer she because it's not yet socially acceptable for boys to dress as girls. After I had that point driven home rather forcefully, I made that choice for my own safety." Lana laughed. "Plus it's easier for the dwarfs to stick to just one. If gender exists on a continuum, I fall more to the feminine side. I like to walk an androgynous line. I am Lana and Roland all the time. But the clothing I choose to wear has nothing to do with me being gay."

"Well, I know that. I'm an equal-opportunity fucker myself."

"What would you call yourself? Bisexual?"

"I've always thought of myself as ambisextrous."

"Neither of us are walking in lockstep with the general population, are we?"

"But you've mastered doing it in heels," Daniel pointed out.

"I should have told you that first day at Henri's, but 20/20 hindsight."

"You should've. We could have been on our two months and a half anniversary by now."

"Oh, are you saying you wouldn't have blinked an eye?"

"I didn't when you told me, remember? You look perfectly normal to me."

"Normal, eh? And what would be abnormal?"

"Oh, maybe if you were a sociopath who liked to have sex with dead bodies after you made them dead. That would be a boner-killer."

"Gross, but you're right. Total boner-killer."

"Yep. But you are most definitely not, even though you're killing me in a different way." Daniel shifted to make room for his filling cock.

"Something is coming up between us."

"Very observant. Which way do you go?"

"Excuse me?"

"Top or bottom?"

Lana stared at him incredulously. "Look at me. Which way do you think I go?"

"You can't judge a book by its cover." Daniel shook with laughter. "And I didn't! I don't know when I'll ever get a chance to say that at a more appropriate time. But you really can't tell by looking. I once knew a very queen-like twink who was a tiger in bed. Only topped. Or so I heard."

Lana's lips curved in a feral smile. "Well, since you ask, I'm flexible. Very flexible."

"I was kind of hoping."

"But I'll bet you mostly top, don't you?"

"Mostly, although I have my moments of flexibility as well. Let me just say this now and this goes for all times, if you don't want to fuck, we don't have to."

Grateful that Daniel put it out there so openly, Lana ran a finger along the curve of his cock. "Your argument for fucking is very persuasive. It's been a long time."

Daniel seemed fixated on her last sentence. He put his hand over Lana's to still it. "How long exactly?"

Lana looked up at the ceiling while counting in her head. Daniel's hand was warm on hers, but not as hot as his cock was under her hand. Her hole twitched with impatience and she gave up the mental gymnastics. "God, I don't know. Nine years or so?"

Daniel shook his head and frowned.

"Does that thundercloud on your face mean you're not going to fuck me?"

He looked up and laughed. "No, I really, really want to fuck you. I just don't know what those guys who walked away were thinking. Sorry, didn't mean to wreck the mood."

Lana shook off his hand and gave his cock another stroke. "Doesn't appear to be completely wrecked."

He moved her hand off his cock and lifted it to his lips. His mouth was hot on the inside of Lana's wrist. When he rolled onto his side to face her, she raised one leg and wrapped it around his waist. Daniel stroked down the length of her flank to caress her hip. He kissed her and slid his hand between her cheeks.

Daniel disentangled their arms. "Onto your stomach, babe."

When she rolled over, she felt Daniel's hands on her shoulders, caressing her from shoulders to waist and then kneading her cheeks firmly. The mattress dipped under her when he straddled her.

He nestled his hard length between her buttocks as he massaged her neck and shoulders. Lana popped her ass up to entice him. Daniel obligingly dragged his cock up and down over her hole with excruciating deliberation.

"You're just teasing me now," she mumbled, her voice muffled by the pillow.

"Mmm-hmm, that's just what I'm doing, luring you to your doom." Daniel's chuckle vibrated against her back. Then his warmth disappeared. "On your hands and knees."

Hopefully, Lana raised her ass into the air and rested her head on her hands, waiting a little nervously for the coming invasion.

Instead she let out a yelp of surprise at the most amazing sensation of a hot wet tongue circling her hole. "Oh my God, what are—" She pushed back and felt him grab her hips, holding her in place. Which was a good thing, as she didn't want to break his nose by accident and her muscles were twitching out of control. She squirmed and jerked her hips at the sensation of his tongue working her open.

She knew she was moaning but heard nothing other than the drumbeat of her heart. Then the warm wetness of his tongue was gone and a slick finger penetrated her.

More than ready, Lana gasped at the slow press of his finger. The initial entry burned a bit, but she wanted more and pushed back against him.

Daniel worked his finger around inside the ring of muscle. When he found her prostate, she let out a soft yelp. "Holy fuck!"

He added a second finger and scissored them to stretch her. "Is this all right?"

"Fuck… now…." Her brain short-circuited from the stimulation. She started to ride his fingers, pushing back hard against his hand.

A shaky chuckle penetrated her sensual fog. "Breathe, baby. Let me know when you're ready."

Lana gathered herself enough to deliver an entire sentence. "Will you just stick the damn thing in?"

Daniel laughed through his panting breaths. "Yes, I would be more than happy to. Told you I'd make you beg."

"Now, Daniel, fuck me right now!"

Daniel pulled his hand away. "Roll over onto your back, babe. I want to see those beautiful eyes when we make love."

Lana flopped onto her back, legs spread invitingly wide. She never thought watching a man put on a condom could be sexy, but knowing his arousal was for her made it unbearably hot. He sank his teeth into his lower lip and squeezed the base of his cock, to get control.

He walked on his knees between her legs. She lifted a leg up over his shoulder, and he responded by pulling her up onto his thighs.

"Ooh," she yelped.

"You like being manhandled a little in the heat of the moment?"

"Perhaps just a little." She grinned at him and thrust her hips up.

But Daniel's face was completely serious. "I won't take it too far. You tell me to stop and everything stops right then."

"I'm telling you to go already," Lana growled in frustration.

"Bold. I like that." He pushed her other leg to the side, spreading her wide open. He leaned down to kiss her, and their cocks bumped between them.

"Damn right."

"You want me to fuck you?"

"Yeah."

"You'll have to beg."

Lana grabbed Daniel's hips, yanking him closer and thrusting up against him. "Listen, buster, you fuck me now and pretty damn quick or—"

"Or what? I told you you'd be begging." Daniel laughed.

"That was ordering, and I'm not the one who'll be begging when I walk out that door!" Lana threatened.

"All right, all right, I know when I'm licked."

"Speaking of licking...."

"Later, babe."

Lana was laughing, but when Daniel slid inside her, all laughter stopped. She'd forgotten the thrill of that burning stretch, but it felt so good. She hissed out a breath at the pleasure of feeling him inside her.

Daniel ducked his head to tongue a nipple and she gasped. "Breathe, baby."

The initial penetration flirted briefly with pain before it tipped over into pleasure. She ran her hands up Daniel's arms, feeling them shudder as he held himself very still. His hands gripped her hips so hard Lana thought tomorrow morning she might feel where each fingertip dug in. "Daniel, please...."

Taking that for permission, Daniel pulled back slightly and then pushed in deeper until his groin was pressed tight up to her balls. The moment she nodded, he began to move slowly.

Daniel had the most incredible expression on his face as he began to move faster, sliding in and out. She didn't want to miss any part of this miracle, still astounded that this man could actually desire her this much.

When Daniel changed his angle slightly, Lana threw her head back and closed her eyes, swept away by her own pleasure. Each time Daniel brushed over the right spot, she tightened her muscles around him, and each time she heard their moans mingle with each exhalation.

His cock swelled inside her, stretching her even more, and then he shifted his weight. Daniel reached for her cock, pumping in time to his thrusts. Then Daniel's rhythm changed. He lost control, driving into Lana harder and faster.

She was so painfully close. Her body went rigid as she quivered on the edge before she was falling and falling and convulsing around Daniel's cock. Lana cried out his name as she came. And then he was coming too, thrusting hard inside her one final time.

He came down onto her in slow motion. As their chests pressed together, heaving for air, the movement tickled when their skin slid together.

"Your prince has come, Snow White," Daniel gasped.

When Lana laughed, she felt his cock soften, and she clamped down, hoping to hold him inside her for a little longer, but he slipped out with a slight sound. She wrapped her arms and legs around him, needing this closeness.

"Yes, you're very… flexible," he panted out.

"Yes, I am." She kissed the side of his neck, the only spot she could reach without letting go.

He turned his head and kissed her on the mouth. "Don't worry. You can schedule a repeat performance anytime and I'll be happy to deliver."

Exhausted and on the edge of sleep, Lana laughed. "Love you."

"Love *you*," Daniel whispered. "Love this, love all of you."

DANIEL OPENED his eyes slowly. Lana was asleep, melted against him like a cat soaking up warmth from a hot stone in winter, her legs still tangled with his.

He spotted the marks his fingers had left and stroked her hip in regret. Regret but also pride. Who knew that deep down he'd wanted to leave marks on her after all. The primal drive to call her *his*, to bare his teeth at any and all competitors, took him by surprise. Never felt that way about anyone before. But he didn't want to hurt Lana to do it, especially after she'd already been hurt so profoundly by that bastard who assaulted her.

Daniel noticed her eyes were open and she was watching him. Lana looked down as he fitted his fingers over each mark in silent atonement.

"Stop me next time if I hurt you." His voice was gruff with shame.

Lana put her hand over his. "You didn't hurt me. Trust me, you have no idea how loud I can scream if I want something to stop."

"I'm still sorry. Sort of." A smile fought past the rigid clench of his jaw, and Daniel gave in to it.

"So proud of yourself." Lana laughed at him as if she could read his thoughts on his face. "We smell."

"I think it's mostly me." Daniel sat up to peel the condom off, cold and sticky now. "I can offer you either a shower or a bath."

"Do you have a hair dryer?"

"No, I'll get one tomorrow. What kind?"

"Then I'll have a bath. I don't like to sleep with wet hair. Takes forever to dry."

"Your wish is my command, but we'll have to use the bathroom in the hall. The en suite only has a shower."

She stretched on the bed and moaned. "You might have to carry me."

"God, I did hurt you!"

"I'm kidding!" Lana sat up and pushed her hair back over her shoulders. "I'm just a little stiff from falling asleep twisted up like a pretzel, but it was great exercise, especially after that huge dinner."

"Is that all it was? A good workout?"

"More attaboys?" Lana raised her brows. "You know it was more than that. Now go make me some hot water."

"Yes, princess. Your wish is my command."

173

He went to the hall bathroom and started the water running. Daniel looked into the cabinet and discovered he had no bubble bath. Not a shock, really, considering he'd never even taken a bath in this apartment, nor had he ever contemplated a fancy one with bubbles.

"First time for everything." He stepped into the bath to test the temperature and sat down. Maybe he should take a bath more often. The warm water felt good, and he was a bit sore from all the activity. He leaned back and rested his arms along the edges.

Lana came in wearing Daniel's robe again, but this time she'd left it hanging open. She'd used the sash to tie up her hair.

The scent of steam and sex almost got Daniel hard again, or maybe it was looking at Lana when she dropped the robe. "Care to join me?"

"I thought you'd never ask." Lana held on to the sink for balance as she stepped into the tub.

After she shut off the water, Daniel pulled her back to lean against him. "Use me as a cushion."

"You're much softer than the tub," she said.

"We aim to please."

Lana snuggled back against him. "And you did. I can't wait to do it again. That was… simply glorious."

Her hair tickled his shoulder. Daniel smiled even though she couldn't see it. "I never knew what a difference love could make. I mean sex is pretty great anytime—"

"But making love is something special." Lana twisted her neck to glance up at him. "That was the first time for me too."

"Another thing we have in common." He brushed a curl out of her face. "I never felt anything this powerful until I met you. First I wanted you because you're beautiful, but now I want you because you're you."

"Complete acceptance?"

He caught the unsure note in her voice. "Yeah. Even if I snore."

After a moment of surprise, Lana laughed and smacked Daniel's knee. "Now wait just a minute! That's asking a bit too much."

"You beautiful idiot." Daniel bent to kiss Lana but could only reach her cheek.

"Imbécile!" Lana mumbled, but she turned in the bath to kiss Daniel back.

CLEAN AND dry after the bath, Daniel pulled on some jeans. "I'm hungry again."

"We have plenty of leftovers."

"Probably enough for a few days. If we're lucky, we won't have to go out for food the entire rest of the weekend." Daniel leered at her. "Leaves time for more important activities."

"Until Monday, when I have to go to work."

"I suppose we'll both be wrung out by then and need time to recover. Care to join me in a snack?" Daniel held out his hand to her.

"I would be charmed as long as I'm not the snack. I don't think I could get it up again for a while." She put on his robe and released her hair from the sash so she could secure the robe around her waist. Then she took his hand.

"Does that mean you're hungry?"

"Hungry and curious." She waited until they were in the kitchen. "That wasn't your first time fucking a boy."

Daniel put the leftovers in the microwave. "I thought I told you that earlier. I've done both."

"Or your second or even the tenth. You know what you're doing." She perched on the lone stool, resting her bare feet on the crossbar.

Poking fun at himself, he puffed out his chest, secretly proud that he'd given her pleasure. "Yeah, I'm good. Would you believe I'm just naturally gifted in the sack?"

"Sure, but I'd also like to hear about how you honed your craft. Shall I bring out the bright lights and shine them in your eyes?"

"No, I'll talk. It's just—" He heaved a big sigh.

"Look, I already heard the worst part, right? How bad could it be?"

"I'm afraid you'll think twice about taking up with me."

"I've already taken up with you. We're past that part. Dom said you're from New York City."

He appreciated Lana's effort to smooth the way for him. "Didn't start there. I was born in beautiful downtown Preble in upstate New York, but then my parents moved in search of a job. I grew up in a small city I'm sure you've never heard of."

"So you were a hick?" Lana laughed.

"Oh boy, was I ever. Backward trucker cap, jeans ripped out at the knees, sleeves cut off my T-shirts, rusted-out pickup truck rattling with empty beer cans, the works."

"And your parents?"

"They're dead. They—drank. Died in a car accident."

"How did you become an artist?"

Daniel laughed out loud. "When I was a kid, I was always drawing and painting. A buddy's dad had a body shop, and I started airbrushing naked women on vans. Or space scenes or vampires, flesh-eating mermaids, you name it. Whatever a customer could dream up, I could paint it. I think I still have a few photos somewhere. I'll try to dig them up. You'd get a kick out of them."

"You must have been good to make it all the way to New York."

"Actually the opposite. The Big Apple came to me."

"Tell me." Lana accepted a plate of food from him and picked up a fork.

Daniel rested his cheek against the top of her head briefly and then moved to serve himself. "I was a horny asshole, and I figured out early on my door swung both ways. Even in a small town, you can always find some secret man-on-man action. But no one ever took off their clothes, so I hate to admit it but I didn't have that much experience when I met him—the guy from the city, I mean."

"Experience in what?"

"Either. Both. Fucking and painting."

"How'd you meet?" she asked when his silence stretched on.

"His name was Tim Madison. He used to come upstate in the summer to do some landscape painting. He saw a couple of my masterpieces and came down to the shop to meet me. You can imagine how the guys laughed behind his back. He was so gay, and in a way that was really, really easy to figure out. I had to bust a few heads when the guys at the shop found out he was looking for me."

"He came to see you?"

"He saw some of my work driving around town, found out who I was, and told me I had talent. Said I should take lessons. Gave me his card, told me if I ever got down to the city, to come and see him." Daniel shrugged and chewed another bite.

"The kind of lessons I think he was thinking about, or real painting lessons?" Lana gave him a sly smile.

"Both." Daniel grinned at the memory. "And even though he was kind of on the wispy side, he was hot and I was up for it. I think I surprised the hell out of him, though, when I showed up on his doorstep in Manhattan."

"What did he do?"

"He allowed me to stay in a spare room in his house. He was a sharp dresser and sophisticated where I was a little bit rough around the edges, but I was young and hot, if I do say so myself. Actually, he said so." His smile slipped. "I guess I was his boy toy, but it wasn't just sex. He let me watch him paint. In a couple of weeks, I was painting too. Wasted a lot of paper, but Tim didn't mind. He really believed in me. Took me with him to art galleries and museums and gave me an education in art history. I—I cared about him. I didn't want to be a drag on him, so I got a part-time job in one of the galleries, which paid shit, but I lost the trucker cap and learned how to dress and how to talk to the kind of people who have the money to buy art."

"And he took you to bed?"

"Yes, it was quite an experience. Tim was a world away from what I was used to. Older experienced man, raw young kid. Of course I was a tough guy and I wasn't going to let him see how insecure I really was. He'd just laugh whenever I felt the need to swing my dick around. But I was lucky. Tim had a lot of experience, and he was just a great guy, really kind. He spent quality time teaching me. And he was versatile, so it could go either way when we hit the sack. I learned a lot from Tim." Daniel's chin started to quiver, and he clenched his teeth to make it stop. He hadn't thought about Tim in a long time.

"Sounds like maybe you did love him a little bit, no matter what kind of love it was."

The idea surprised Daniel, but it didn't feel wrong. He nodded slowly. "Maybe I did, although I never could have admitted it back then. Maybe he knew, but we never mentioned the word. I know I owe him a lot."

"Do you still keep in touch?"

"He died. HIV." Daniel hunched his shoulders against the pain. "That was bad. We'd always played it safe fooling around and I was okay, but I took care of Tim until he went into the hospital. After he was gone, I was on my own. I had to start earning my own way or go back to painting vans upstate. Once I had a taste of the city, I didn't want to go back to the sticks. The executor of Tim's will was a friend of his, and he knew about me. He let me live in the house until all Tim's business was settled, but then I was out on my own."

"What did you do?"

"I still had a job at the gallery, and one day this rich society wife kind of came on to me. I didn't get her approach at first, probably too subtle for a hick like me. I'd been so wrapped up in Tim, the door only swung one way for a while. But she asked if I would paint her portrait. Well, I was flattered. The next big artist, right? I said yes but I didn't have any place to paint. She set me up in a little place in Chelsea with enough room for a studio, and she paid the bills."

"So you were a kept man."

"Earning my keep." Daniel shoveled in a bite and chewed. "It didn't bother me at all at the time. She would come by during the day for sittings, so my nights were free and I did whatever I wanted. Or whoever."

"Sittings, eh?"

Heat burned his face. Daniel stared down at his plate. "At first it was sittings. Man, this sounds a lot worse than it seemed. I was used to making it with a guy, so I guess maybe I was a little rough around the edges, but she liked it and kept coming back for more. Then her husband got suspicious."

"Did you get in trouble?"

"I really did want to paint her portrait, if only to prove that Tim hadn't been wasting his time on me. One day her husband showed up unexpectedly. Luckily we were done with the fucking and had gotten back to the painting. She told him the portrait was a present for his birthday. He liked the look of it, even though he didn't like the look of me. From then on, he came along to supervise and she used to stare at me like a parched dog with an empty water dish. He stood propped against the wall looking over my shoulder. Looking back and forth between her and the canvas." Daniel shook his head at the memory. "Let me tell you, that is the *worst* way to paint, but I got it done. He shelled out, took her and the painting away, and that was the end of that."

"And you never saw her again?"

Daniel grinned. "I saw her all the time at the gallery. She would stare at me longingly and sigh, and I would try to avoid her. But she did me a favor. She must have told a friend about my 'skills,' and the friend came looking to get a portrait done and to get done herself. And she was willing to pay for it too."

"So you were able to live off your painting?"

"In a manner of speaking. At first I was heavily subsidized by my sideline, but I would have done just about anything to never paint another sexy babe on a van. For a long time, I had no complaints and all the action I could handle. They liked me fucking them but treated me like I had an On/Off switch. Believe it or not, after a while it was stressful having to whip it up on command."

"So what did you do?"

"I went back to fucking boys at night. No strings. No performance anxiety. Just straight-up physical release." Daniel shook his head at himself.

"How did you get into the blackmail?"

"You had to ask." Daniel's smile faded.

"You told me I could ask you anything."

"I did. I'm not proud of this."

Lana put her hand on his. "You don't have to talk about it until you're ready. Maybe never."

Daniel nodded. After all, he'd let her off the hook in a similar way. Some scars were just too fresh. "Thanks."

"Why didn't you tell the dwarfs all this?"

"I had reasons for what I did, but that doesn't excuse it. It was wrong."

"I know. But we don't always do the right thing. I didn't tell you about me when I should have." Lana's voice was soft. Soothing.

"Tim wouldn't have approved of me in those years. He was an actual gentleman, in the best sense of the word, but not me. Some of those women weren't so nice. Neither were their husbands. I guess I thought they deserved it." From the look in Lana's eyes, Daniel could tell she didn't despise him. He was grateful for that. He despised himself enough for both of them.

"You can't be a whore for years and not have it affect you. The first affair was a surprise to me. Didn't blackmail her. Hell, I was grateful to her. But some of the other women treated me like dirt." He laughed bitterly. "I can't tell you what a rush it was, the first time I did it. She hated me, but she paid. And I liked that she was hating me. It was better than sex. The perfect revenge. Just a little more dirt splashing up on me. By then I didn't think I was worth anyone's love, so what the fuck."

"But Tim thought you were and I do too, so we're right," Lana said.

Daniel stood up and took their empty plates to the dishwasher. Then he turned to face her, almost unbearably moved by her faith in him. "I could get used to this."

"You and me?" Lana stood up and came to him. She put her arms around him, and he held her close.

"You and me. I've never brought anyone else here. In fact, I haven't had sex since I've been here in Paris. Aside from whacking off, of course."

"Of course." Suppressed laughter vibrated in her voice.

"Thanks for listening. I never thought anyone would again. Not like I deserve it."

"You deserve it," Lana said softly. "I know how it feels to be on your own."

"You can't possibly know how big a deal this is for me."

Lana leaned back to look at him. "I think we're in the same boat."

"Your secret wasn't technically illegal."

"True, just morally repugnant to some."

"Not to me. I kinda like it." Daniel grinned. "So I guess we're stuck with each other now."

"No one I'd rather be stuck with." Lana stood on tiptoes to kiss him and then yawned.

"Tired? Four times in one day is almost a record for me."

"Almost?" Lana yawned again. "Now that I've eaten, I'm exhausted."

"Let's go to bed."

His arm wrapped tightly around her, they climbed the stairs together.

CHAPTER 11

DANIEL WOKE up happy. When he turned his head to see Lana lying on her stomach, fast asleep, the sight made him even happier.

Moving carefully, Daniel leaned over to kiss her bare shoulder. Lana's skin was smooth and warm, and he was tempted to take a nibble. Lana let out a tiny contented snort but didn't move. More pressing matters like the state of his bladder drove Daniel out of bed. After that and a quick shower, he propped himself against the doorframe of his bedroom, gloating over the beautiful sight.

He remembered he had nothing in the house for breakfast except leftovers from last night's takeaway. Chinese for breakfast didn't appeal, and he had plans for the rest of the day, which meant Lana had to be well fed and energetic. Daniel dressed and went down the stairs quietly. He picked up his wallet and keys and left, locking the door behind him.

The rain had stopped during the night, and the early rays of sun made the honey-colored stone of the buildings gleam like gold. Overnight everything seemed to have become mysteriously more beautiful and vibrant. The delicious aroma of baking bread and fresh coffee drew him to his usual boulangerie, and he went in to buy breakfast.

The sight of three short men standing in front of his building brought him up short, and Daniel chuckled. They all turned to watch him as he approached. "Good morning, gentlemen. Here to check up on me?"

Terry started. "Where is—"

"Lana." Dom cut in without ceremony. "Where is she?"

"I assume Lana is still asleep. She was when I went out to get breakfast." Daniel unlocked the outer door and led the way upstairs to his flat.

Colin sniffed at the package under Daniel's arm. "Good bread."

"Don't worry, I got enough for all of us." Daniel led the way into his kitchen and put the paper sack on the table. Although yesterday he'd been worrying about the lack of dining table and chairs, today's uninvited guests gave him a laugh at the thought of the impending competition to cop the lone stool in the kitchen. "Would anyone like to volunteer to make the coffee?"

Colin was unpacking the bag. He muttered approvingly to himself as he pulled out butter and a jar of preserves. "Do you have a basket and a linen towel I can use to keep these rolls warm?"

Daniel pointed at a cupboard. "Help yourself. I think you'll find all you need."

"Better let Lana make the coffee," Dom said. "She makes the best coffee I've ever tasted."

"Hey!" Colin surfaced from inside the cupboard. "I'm the one who taught her how to make coffee, remember?"

"And that's the only thing you taught her. She sure can't make a pot of tea fit for consumption." Terry reached for a roll and winced when Colin slapped his hand away.

"Wait for Lana."

"I'll go see if she's awake." Daniel went toward the stairs.

"Better set off a bomb," Dom called after him. "She's a heavy sleeper."

Weird that they knew her better than he did, but he knew a different side of her they never would. Daniel could hear the babble of the dwarfs arguing as he went up the stairs, but not exactly what they were saying. He closed the door to the bedroom to shut out the sound. Lana was still asleep, her body completely relaxed on the bed.

Daniel bent to brush the hair out of Lana's face. "How are you this morning?"

"Slightly sore but insatiable. Where were you?" Lana spoke without opening her eyes. "You went away."

"I went out to get breakfast." Daniel sat on the edge of the bed and stroked her arm. "When I returned, we were invaded by dwarfs."

Lana rolled onto her back and stared up at the ceiling. "Fuck them sideways with a pogo stick. No morning quickie?"

Daniel busted out laughing. "Speaking of insatiable, I think I may have met my match, but we'll have time later. They came to see if you're okay, and they want you to make the coffee. I don't think they're going anywhere until they see you."

"You're probably right, and they do admit I make good coffee." Lana looked around the room blankly. "Can I borrow something to wear? I don't see my clothes."

"How about what you have on now?" Daniel teased. "You look perfect to me."

"Too cold." Lana lifted the blanket and peeked down at herself. "If I go down like this, there will be a lot of size-matters jokes and you'll feel impelled to defend my honor."

"And we don't want that. Despite the obvious disadvantages of your entourage, I rather like the dwarfs because they love you." Daniel rubbed Lana's groin lightly through the blanket. "Although I'll have them know I have no complaints on the score of size."

"Stop it." Lana pushed his hand away. "There are some things one's friends should never see, and me waving a woody around is one of them."

"I'll get your clothes from the dryer." Daniel tilted Lana's face up and kissed him on the lips. "And I'll grind some coffee beans for you."

Lana groaned as she sat up. "I had to go and buy a dwarf alarm clock."

Daniel laughed and then watched Lana until the bathroom door closed behind her before he went back downstairs to join the dwarfs.

"She'll be right down." Daniel was interested to note that Terry had commandeered the lone stool while Dom stood glowering at him. Daniel collected Lana's clothing from the dryer and went back upstairs. The water was running in the bathroom, so he left her clothes on the bed where she would see them and returned to the kitchen.

Completely at home in the kitchen, Colin was setting places on the table. "Hope you don't mind my raiding your pantry." He had set out the milk for the coffee, plates, flatware, and napkins. "Although there wasn't much to raid."

"I don't mind at all now that we're in-laws." Daniel grinned at their startled expressions. He leaned against the counter and crossed his arms. "I have no secrets from you guys anymore."

Terry snickered. "I'll just bet you do." Clearly taking no chances of losing his seat, Terry leaned way over from the stool to poke Daniel in the ribs.

"You're right, some things must always remain...." Daniel looked up when he caught a movement on the upper stair. Even in plain, boring, and completely neutral socks, just the sight of Lana's feet stepped up his heart rate. "Damn," he muttered. He was so lost.

LOOKING UP to find out why Daniel's jaw went slack, Dom raised his hand to cover a smirk. Lana, of course. He'd never seen that satisfied look on her face before. And the way she searched for Daniel in the room and the smile that lit her face when she saw him... well, Dom suddenly discovered he had something in his eye and rubbed it vigorously.

"Hello, boys." Lana gave them a smug grin before she drifted over to the coffeemaker. Poetry in motion as she put in the filter, poured in the water, and measured the grounds. She was flying. Lana went to lean on the counter next to Daniel and snuggled closer to him. He put his arm around her. "Looks like we have company, honey."

Her smile when she looked at Daniel was infinitely more radiant than when she'd smiled at her old friends.

Dom cleared his throat. "We came to make sure you're okay."

"I don't think you have to worry about me anymore, Happy." Lana didn't look away from Daniel's face.

Daniel was beaming at her, obviously equally besotted and happy.

Lana had not buttoned her collar tight to her throat as she usually did, and the scars were obvious in the morning light.

185

"You look beautiful, Lana." After watching them together, Dom was finally able to relax. Maybe she really was going to be okay. Love shimmered in the air like an aura. Or maybe it was just the way the sunlight came in the window.

"Thank you, Dom. Coffee's ready." Lana slipped out of Daniel's embrace and went to get the pot.

Still trying to divine the man's inner thoughts, Dom watched Daniel watching her as she poured coffee for everyone.

"How did you all meet?" Daniel took a sip of his coffee, never taking his gaze off Lana.

Dom looked at Terry and Colin, and they giggled naughtily. Still the Musketeers.

"Lana didn't tell you?"

"She said you met at school and you protected her from the bullies," Daniel answered. "I'd like to hear your side of it."

"Colin and Terry lived next door to each other, so they were friends already," Dom started. "The rest of us all met in kindergarten."

"Even then, Lana was a beanpole," Colin said.

"Taller than any of us and stayed that way," Terry added. "The boys didn't like how feminine she was and the girls didn't like her because she was so much prettier."

"She was picked on a lot." Dom smacked a fist into his cupped hand. "I didn't like that, so I said, stick with us and we'll—"

"He started taking out my five-year-old enemies." Lana smiled at Dom, and he smiled back.

"And we all just hit it off," Terry said.

"We were the guard and she was the princess." Colin helped himself to another roll and anointed it liberally with butter.

"A princess in a checked shirt and corduroys," Lana said. "I didn't get to choose my own outfits back then."

"But we knew," Terry said.

"If Lana was feminine even then, how did you all feel about that?" Daniel asked.

"What did we know? She was fun and that's all we cared about," Colin said.

"She's still a lot of fun." Daniel wiggled his brows at Lana. She fluttered her lashes at him as she slowly turned pink.

"Colin has an older sister who was a tomboy. So we decided Lana was a tomgirl." Dom shrugged. "Made sense to our five-year-old minds."

"So we hung out and took our vows as Musketeers—"

Lana cut in. "And princess."

"And princess." Colin nodded at her. "And we stayed friends and we always will. The end."

"When her parents kicked her out, we tried to help as much as we could," Terry said. "She would have done the same for us."

"And the attack?" Daniel looked sorry as soon as the question was out.

Lana looked up at the ceiling and compressed her lips tightly.

"Lana doesn't like talking about it," Dom said.

"Thanks, Dominick," Lana said softly.

"Neither does Dom," Terry said, a protective note in his voice.

Dom looked at him in surprise. "Thanks, Terry." He turned to Lana. "I'm sorry I had to call your parents."

"I know, Dom, don't worry about it. What else could you do? We were fifteen." Lana reached out and squeezed Dom's hand. "I'm not mad about it. I never was."

He kept her hand in his for a moment. "At least you're all right."

"We never thought she'd end up dating anyone." Colin used the tip of his finger to pick up the crumbs from his plate and licked them off.

"And then you come along and blow her socks off." Dom pointed an accusing finger and then was startled by Daniel and Lana's laughter.

"Sorry." Daniel recovered first. "Just a running joke."

"A match made in heaven. They have inside jokes already."

"Lana told me about her job writing about socks."

"Socks?" Brows raised, the dwarfs looked at one another and shrugged.

Lana raised her brows in pride. "My first published paragraph was about socks."

"So anyway, Lana is one of us, and anyone who hurts her hurts all of us." Dom leaned forward to stare menacingly at Daniel. "If *you* do, Mr. Daniel Hunter, we'll hunt you down, chop off your balls, and feed them to the wolves."

Lana laughed. "No ball chopping until you check with me first, do you read me, dwarfs?"

Finally Dom grinned. "I think everyone reads you loud and clear, Lana. You kids have my blessing."

"Kids?" Lana protested indignantly.

Daniel set down his cup and put his arms around her. "Don't look a gift horse in the mouth."

ON MONDAY Lana was seated at her desk, leaning her head in her hand, dreamily thinking over every last detail of what she and Daniel had done that weekend and not doing a lick of work. When Catharine knocked on the door, Lana straightened up and tried to look busy.

Catharine bustled into Lana's office, holding up the latest issue of the magazine to show off the cover. "Hot off the presses. Your Haute Macabre editorial from the photo shoot. I think it turned out fabulous."

"Thanks." Lana reached for it eagerly. The fun of seeing her work in print still hadn't worn off, and she hoped it never would. "Cool." She flipped the pages over, smiling in delight. She would study it later.

"Looks like *someone* had a very good weekend. I would say something more, but we're at work, if you get my drift, even though I would welcome any details you care to share. Would Daniel be wearing that same smug grin this morning? And perhaps very little else?"

Lana knew she was blushing and she just couldn't stop grinning a grin that never ended, but she said, "Be quiet, Catharine. If I told you everything that happened, you'd probably cover your ears and run screaming into the night."

"I'm broad-minded, I am, and night is hours away. I can stand up to hearing about whatever it is you two got up to. And whatever you did, I hope it was suitably naughty." Catharine rubbed her hands together with satisfaction, but then she gave Lana a genuine smile. "I'm just glad to see you happy at last. You've spent too long alone."

Her face cooling, Lana said, "I am happy. Happier than I ever thought possible."

"So when do I get to meet him? Or does that hickey on your neck mean your nights are booked until next year?"

Hickey? Lana scrambled for the mirror she kept in her desk. She hadn't even noticed when she put on her makeup—

"I don't have a hickey!"

"Made you look!" Catharine laughed. "I guess if the weather wasn't hot and steamy where you were, you wouldn't have had to check in a panic."

"I did not panic." Lana tried to stay on her dignity, but that grin that wouldn't stop was back. "I can tell you that we had a very nice time, thank you for asking."

Catharine held up her hands in defeat, but she was still laughing. "I can take a hint. Just let me say I'm very happy for you, and tell Daniel if he doesn't treat you as you deserve to be treated, he'll have me to deal with."

"I'll tell him, but you'll have to stand in line behind the dwarfs."

CHAPTER 12

FOR THE first time in longer than he could remember, Dom actually looked forward to meeting Lana for lunch. He loved her, but the constant worry and guilt he'd borne since the attack got in the way of their friendship. Now it was finally melting away. A weight off his shoulders. In fact, from suspecting Daniel of ulterior motives, Dom had swung around to the other side. He'd never seen Lana happier, and he might just need to thank Daniel for that.

When he walked into Henri's café, Lana was already there waiting for him. Henri waved a greeting and came to their table.

After Henri had taken their order, Lana asked, "How're things with Gilles?"

Dom leaned back in the booth and gave her a lascivious smirk. "Couldn't be better, if you get my drift." He waggled his eyebrows.

"So he got over suspecting you of having an affair with me, which was only reasonable on his part considering the amount of time you spent following me around?"

"He thought I was a bisexual cheating heel seeing you on the sly, until you agreed to meet him, which I thank you for." Dom looked around, but none of the other customers seemed interested. "You didn't have to tell him about, uh, you know."

"I know you really love Gilles, and I didn't want to cause problems between you. I didn't mind telling him. He was very nice about it. Besides, once you're married, he'll have to know anyway, won't he? If we're all for one, we also have to be one for all."

"Who said anything about getting married?"

"You're a fraud, Dom. I know you think he's the one."

On the defense, Dom tried a parry. "And what about Daniel? Are you sure he's the one for you?"

"I'm sure."

"What's he doing when you're at work?"

"He's painting again. He's got two commissions for portraits."

Dom had never seen Lana's face like this. Before she'd always been tightly wound, vigilant for her safety, aside from when she was alone with him and the other Musketeers. Now she radiated newly found confidence. "Listen, I know I'm about to offend you, but if anything ever goes wrong between you and Daniel, you know we'll always be there for you."

"It's probably just become a habit with you. You've been looking out for me for so long, Dom, and I appreciate that, but thank goodness you've turned it down a couple of notches."

Dom nodded thoughtfully. "Terry told me I can't be objective about you and to fucking give it a fucking rest for fuck's sake, direct quote, but I just want to be certain. I worry about you."

"People can change, and that includes you and me, as well as Daniel. Almost dying has a way of making you focus on what's important in life. He regrets what he did."

Aware that he did not share their experience, Dom could only nod. "You did nothing to deserve what happened to you. He should regret his actions, considering what he did. But neither of you deserved to almost die."

"I'm not saying Daniel is a perfect man—"

Dom burst into laughter.

She grinned. "Shut up. Going through a traumatic experience and having that in common seems to help. We don't have to talk about every detail, but we both get it."

"I understand."

"We both came out the other side different. I know how you found me and that was horrible for you, but it's not the same as having it actually happen to you. Even if Daniel lied to everyone else, he could never lie to me. We've both stood on the knife's edge, and that's something that never goes away."

Lana had never talked even this much about the assault before. Dom nodded to acknowledge what she said, all his words deserting him.

Lana leaned forward and lowered her voice. "Daniel loves me exactly the way I am. Can't you understand how precious that is?"

Terry was right. He had to let this go. Dom pulled himself together and grinned. "Underwear and all?"

Laughing, Lana held up crossed fingers in the universal antivampire sign. "Not that my underwear is *any* of your business, but yes. He accepts me completely."

Dom sighed. "I don't get it," he said, not for the first time.

Lana said, "I don't get it either. I didn't ask to be made this way, but I like wearing these clothes. I never thought I'd find a man who loved me just as I am and didn't want to change me, but now that I have—"

"You decided to man up and reach for the stars."

Lana giggled. "Well put."

"Have you survived your first fight yet?"

"Have you?"

"I asked first."

"You're still a dick, Dom, but a nice dick." Lana and Dom leaned closer and giggled. "Yes, we had our first fight and came through alive."

"Tears?"

"And screaming and storming out. Two boxes of tissues later, he was rushing over to apologize and ran into me while I was rushing back to—"

"Let me guess. To apologize?" Dom grinned.

Lana nodded. "We worked it out. And it helped me to realize we can argue and he's still going to love me when we get over our snit."

"You never worried when we had a fight."

"We have more history. And the fights weren't exactly about the same thing."

"Neither was the making up later. What did you argue about?"

Lana frowned at him. "None of your business."

"That dumb, huh?"

"How did you know?" Lana giggled and shook her head.

"Ask me what Gilles and I argued about."

"All right, I'm asking."

"You don't want to know, but it was that dumb also, and two boxes of tissues later...." Dom circled his hand in the air. "You know the drill. But once the apologies were out of the way, the make-up sex was pretty hot. So, seriously. How's Daniel rate in the bedroom?"

"None of your business." The smug smile on Lana's face spoke volumes. Dom recognized how that same smirk felt on his own face.

"What does he have to say about your parents?"

"He said he wouldn't condescend to take money from that bunch of intolerant dicks if they offered it."

"Daniel's got his heart in the right place when it comes to you," Dom growled. "Even though dear old Dad deserves all the bad things coming to him."

"Let's not talk about them. I'm just happy I'll never have to see them again." The hurt look disappeared when Lana smiled. "I made my own family, and I'm much happier with my Musketeers and Daniel."

"I'm really happy for you, Lana."

"And I'm glad for you and Gilles."

"No, I mean it. You look happier than I've ever seen you." Dom realized that was the truth. In the past he'd seen Lana ecstatic over an outfit or a work assignment, but nothing else. "At peace."

"I don't have to hide with Daniel."

"And that's the best thing you could ever tell me. I always hoped you'd find your happy ending."

Lana reached forward to touch Dom's arm. "After the attack, I built a dam around my feelings, even though I knew it couldn't hold everything in forever. With Daniel, I don't have to. He knows I'm going to have bad days sometimes, because he has them too. And we'll both be there to help one another when we need it."

She didn't mention nightmares, and Dom wondered if she or Daniel ever woke in the night with a scream, trembling and crying.

Gilles had been there to hold him the last time, and he hoped it was the same for Lana, but he would never ask. The rest of what they shared was bad enough. He didn't want to trigger a bad dream for her too. "So am I invited to the wedding?"

"If we ever decide there'll be one, you can be maid of honor," Lana promised him.

"*Man* of honor," Dom stressed. "So are you seeing him tonight?"

"Yes, I am." Lana's face flushed pink.

"Care to tell me what you're doing? Want to give me and Gilles any pointers, so to speak, if you get what I mean, wink, wink, nod, nod." Dom winked as vigorously as if he had an eyelash in his eye.

"Don't be such a dick." Lana laughed and then assumed a haughty manner to announce grandly, "We are planning to moon the boats on the Seine this evening. I shall be wearing a chic, elegant frock with a fitted bodice and a full circle skirt, perfect for flinging up insouciantly to expose the buttocks to—"

"Oh, keep it a secret, then, don't tell *me*." Dom pouted.

"Don't worry, I wasn't going to."

"Ring me if you guys end up in jail. I'll bail you out. If I'm not too busy to answer the phone." Dom winked at her again.

TONIGHT LANA was wearing a chic minidress, black with red accents on the armholes and pockets, geometric shapes traced out in thin leather lines, and with an asymmetrical wrap skirt. Her makeup was perfect, her hair back in a stylish chignon with some loose curls around her face, and she had on her usual four-inch heels. What didn't show was a luxurious new set of lingerie, a gift from Daniel. He hadn't seen her in them yet, but Lana knew he was going to like the new bra and thong. No stockings or garter belt because it was hot that fall.

Lana opened a window and leaned out to see if Daniel had arrived yet. He waved up at her with a smile, and she blew him a kiss. Then she locked the door to her flat and went down to meet him. Daniel had insisted for the sake of Lana's reputation that he never stay overnight. Charmingly old-fashioned, although Lana had pointed out that it didn't make much difference considering she had no reputation to speak of and stayed over at Daniel's flat six nights out of seven, but he had held firm.

Daniel greeted her with a hug. He always took her in his arms as if she was something precious to be cared for and loved. After they kissed, they held hands as they walked.

"I still can't get over how good you are in those heels."

"Practice, honey.

"The taller they are—"

"Isn't that the bigger they are?"

"We both know who's bigger." Daniel wore a huge shit-eating grin.

"You want to whip it out and compare right now?"

"Better wait until we get home and I will be happy to oblige."

"Where are we going?"

"It's a surprise." Daniel walked her to a taxi stand and opened the door for her. "I thought we'd take a walk down memory lane on our anniversary." He leaned forward to speak to the driver. "Quai des Grand Augustins, s'il vous plaît."

Lana blinked in surprise. "What anniversary is that?"

Daniel looked at his watch. "It's been five months, seventeen days, and almost fourteen hours since we started dating."

"When are you counting from?" Touched, Lana held back a laugh.

"Our second date." Daniel beamed at her. "When you trusted me with the truth. We'll have another anniversary on the day I came clean to you."

"Will that involve the dwarfs?"

"Preferably not, but if you want them to watch, I'll do my best."

Lana shuddered at the thought. "God forbid."

"Good, because I do my best work with an audience of one."

"Hey, I'm not exactly the audience. I'm doing my share." Lana slapped at his shoulder.

He caught her hand and kept it. "And you do excellent work."

She squeezed his hand. "Thank you for noticing. Back to the scene of the crime?"

"I prefer to think of it as one of the greatest love scenes in the history of man."

Lana raised her brows. "And women."

"And women." Daniel bowed to her. "Perhaps I'm being a little grandiose—"

"No perhaps about it."

"—but I can honestly say that was the best night of my entire life."

"Including the night we—"

Daniel put a finger to her lips. "This is about love and finding it when you'd all but given up on it."

Lana nipped at his finger. "I'm just a bit giddy because it was the best love scene I've ever been in. Not to mention the only."

When they arrived at the Seine, Daniel led her across the Pont Neuf bridge. This time they descended with arms linked and Lana cuddled close against him. To her surprise, Daniel had arranged for the same table on the same boat.

Instead of rain, the sun was setting, and the menu was different, but Lana felt the same thrill as the trip began. When they raised their glasses to each other, Lana contrasted the intimacy of their conversation with last time, when they each clutched their secrets. And yet the comfort she felt tonight was shot through with the excitement of that night.

"So what do you think of my idea?"

"Very romantic." Lana hadn't stopped smiling since they got into the taxi. "We should have anniversaries more often."

"I'm game. We can make them up as we go." Daniel raised his glass again. "Happy new underwear day."

"I have them on," Lana whispered. Heat flooded her face, but she grinned.

Daniel waggled his eyebrows. "Dessert?"

"Definitely."

The air was still warm when they disembarked from the boat. They strolled along the Quai de Conti to the Pont des Arts.

"I remember when the railings were covered with padlocks."
Daniel stopped at the center of the bridge under a streetlight.

"Locks of love." Lana ran her hand along the smooth railing.
After the overwhelming mass of locks were removed, the bare glass
panels provided a better view of the river and the boats passing below.
"You weren't planning to add one for us and throw the key into the
Seine, were you?"

"It's a nice gesture, but I had something better in mind." Daniel
went down on one knee in front of Lana, still holding her hand and
looking up at her. "Lana Renault, I am more serious than I've ever
been in my entire life. I love you more than any words I can think up
to tell you, and I will always love you. Loving you has made a better
man of me, and I need you. I'm asking—I'm begging you, will you
marry me?

"Yes, I'll marry you!" She bent to kiss Daniel, holding his face
in her hands.

"Bonsoir, madame et monsieur."

Lana broke the kiss and Daniel scrambled to his feet.

The gendarme who'd spoken just nodded with an understanding
smile and continued on his rounds.

Lana put her hand over her heart to still the pounding. "God, he
surprised me."

"He must be used to it. This is the bridge of love. Maybe he
thought we were an old married couple, back to relive our glory
days," Daniel said.

"Old! Speak for yourself."

"Well, what about it?"

"What about what?"

"Getting married."

"You mean for real? Truly, legally married?" Tonight's roller-
coaster ride just took another exciting swoop.

"It would be sort of the ultimate con, don't you think?" Daniel
said. "When you think of it, we're both in the same sort of sideline to
our main gigs."

Lana sighed. "It would be, wouldn't it?"

"Or we could take a jaunt over to England, if you want to recite the words in your native tongue."

"Hell no. If I marry you, it'll only be for the sake of your bathtub."

"Any reason will do."

Lana threw herself into his arms.

Laughing, Daniel asked, "Don't you even want to see the ring?"

"What ring?"

"It's customary when a man asks another to be his lawful wedded wife—"

"Partner, you lunatic."

"To offer a ring as a sign of good faith or promise or something." Daniel struggled to get the box out of his tight jeans. "Have a look. If you hate it, we'll go and pick out another."

"Cartier?"

"Only the box. The ring is actually out of a crackerjack box, but I wanted to impress you with the name. Open it."

Lana gasped in shock at the sight of the ring. A large emerald blazed green from the center of an ultramodern platinum setting. Two baguette diamonds glittered at either side. "It's gorgeous! I'll take it! And I'll take you! Dom always told me I needed to get myself a rich husband."

"I doubt he actually said that, but if he did, he was right and I'm your man." Daniel slipped the ring onto Lana's finger and put his arm around her. "We'll make plans tomorrow. Who do you want to invite?"

"My friend Catharine and her husband. And the dwarfs, of course, and their mates. I promised Happy he could be maid of honor."

"Dom must have been thrilled by that honor," Daniel said with a chuckle.

"Not so you'd notice it," Lana said. "I think he's afraid I'll pick out a dress he can only wear once."

"With your fashion sense?"

"I know! What *is* he thinking? But he can be man of honor if he prefers."

"As long as we're together," Daniel said.

"Forever," Lana said.

"Let's go home," Daniel said.

Lana kissed him. "Let's, my love."

CATT FORD lives behind the orange curtain in southern California
with a partner and two familiars in the form of cats whose fur is as
black as their evil little hearts. She is a graphic artist by day and a
storyteller by inclination. Catt enjoys the research required for writing
a believable story. She is a rabid card-carrying fan of bull riding and
also enjoys swing dancing. She gets drunk on words and sometimes
overimbibes, but loves to write about love and happy endings.

Blog: catt-ford.livejournal.com

BULLDOZED

Catt Ford

Bull rider Trey Stuart voluntarily ties himself onto the back of a 1,500-pound animal for fun and money. But however tough he is in the ring, Trey is too scared to take a chance on love, especially when the man he wants is star rider Smoke Carter. Trey and Smoke have been hooking up for years, but Trey denies there's anything serious going on between them.

Joining them at the gay rodeo are their friends Dolly and Alex. Wanting the same happiness for their friends, the two women try to convince Trey that Smoke is just as interested in him. While Trey works to help Dolly succeed in covering her first bull, another man tries to come between him and Smoke. When Smoke challenges Trey to cowboy up, he has to decide if the ride is worth the risk.

www.dreamspinnerpress.com

BULLHEADED

Catt Ford

Aging bull rider Cody Grainger needs bullfighter Johnny Arrow for more than just protection in the ring. Their bond of trust goes beyond the professional and into love, but while their relationship holds up to the need for discretion imposed by their sport and repeatedly having to watch each other put themselves in the way of dangerous animals, other barriers still tear them apart.

For one thing, Cody is ten years older than Johnny. But instead of contemplating retirement, he focuses on winning the championship, desperate to stay on top. Johnny is only beginning to find the professional recognition he craves. When frustration leads Johnny to walk away, Cody's season slumps. While they're apart, they both slowly realize they are meant to be together. But machismo abounds in the sport of bull riding, and their pride might be an obstacle too big for love to overcome.

The CAGE

Catt Ford

Welcome to The Cage, where you can share the ups and downs of a group of friends as they enjoy a rollicking adventure of sex and love in "the life."

Being a Dom has always come naturally to Lazar Thornton, owner and operator of The Cage, a thriving adult toy store and meeting place for Lazar's closest friends, Bran, Max, Otto, and the always flamboyant and fierce Miss Dré. But even the best of friends have different tastes in scenes—and in life.

Good-humored and laid back, but much in demand as both teacher and Dom, Lazar has always run from love. Until Ben Owen, relative newbie to the BDSM world, arrives wide-eyed and eager to learn, and Lazar wants to teach this sub everything he knows. But despite the openness needed for a Dom/sub relationship to thrive, neither discusses emotions. Feeling the sting of unrequited love, Ben isn't as sure of his place in Lazar's life as he wants to be. Lazar will need to read his sub's heart as well as his mind if he truly wants to keep Ben in his life.

www.dreamspinnerpress.com

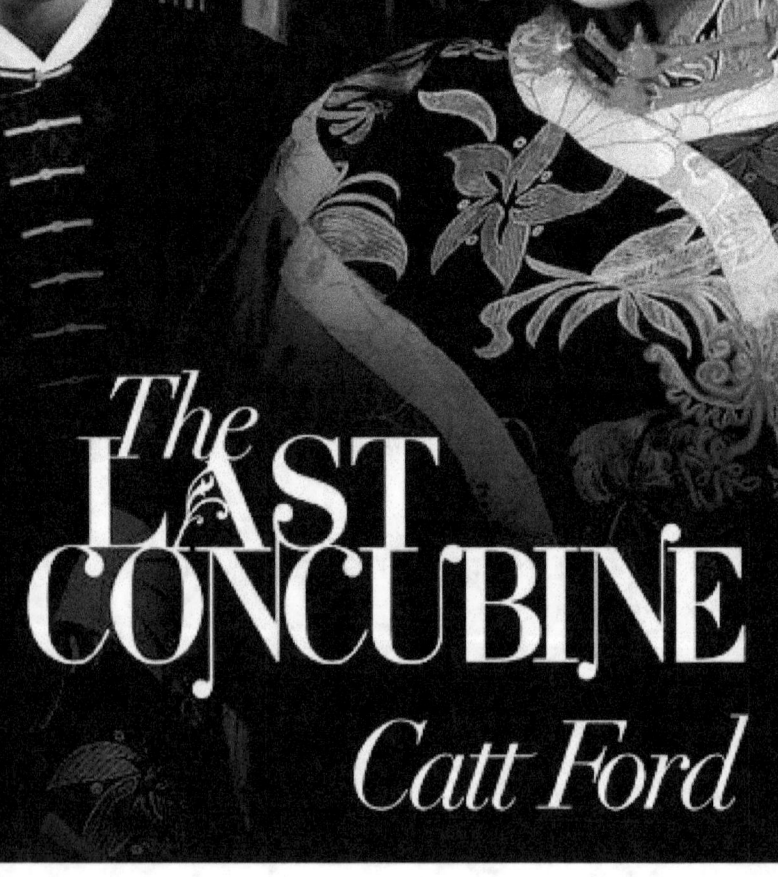

The
LAST
CONCUBINE

Catt Ford

When Princess Lan'xiu's brother delivers her under duress into General Hüi Wei's harem as a political offering, her only question is how soon her secret will be discovered. She is under no illusions: when the general discovers she is actually a he, death is his only future—though he doesn't plan to make it easy. Lan'xiu has dressed as a woman all his life, but he is no damsel in distress. He can swing a sword with the best of them.

General Hüi Wei has everything a man could want: power, wealth, success on the battlefield, and a harem of concubines. At first, he regards Lan'xiu with suspicion, but he finds himself strangely drawn to her. When he discovers the beautiful young woman is actually a man, his first reaction is to draw his sword. Rather than waste such beauty, he decides to enjoy the spirited Lan'xiu's submission—and ignites a passion and desire deeper than anything he's felt with other wives. But court intrigue, political ambitions, and the general's doubts may be too much for their love to overcome.

www.dreamspinnerpress.com

When Texas Ranger Tell Hadley is sent to investigate rustling in Oklahoma Territory, he finds two dead men and signs of a survivor on the run. Were the killings lynchings or simply frontier justice? Tracking the one man left standing leads him to Noel Ivory, a tenderfoot East Coast journalist who claims his friend Jack Rogers was murdered. Neither man trusts the other, and both have secrets to keep, but if they're going to solve the murder at the Rocking R, they're going to have to let down their guards and show their hands.

www.dreamspinnerpress.com